Evil of the Witch Rose

A Father's Love (But Not What You Think)

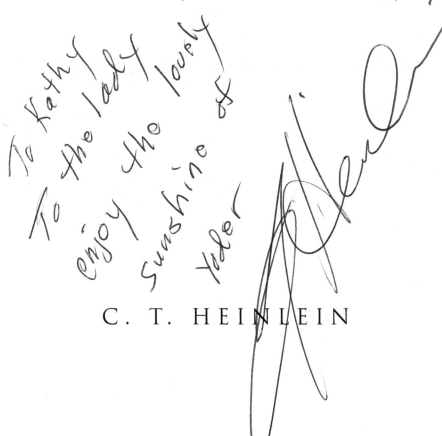

To Kathy
To the lady lovely
enjoy the
sunshine of
Tyler

C. T. HEINLEIN

PAGE PUBLISHING, INC.
New York, NY

First originally published by Page Publishing, Inc. 2018

ISBN 978-1-64214-341-6 (Paperback)
ISBN 978-1-64214-342-3 (Digital)

Printed in the United States of America

Dedicated to
Charlie, my Junior,
who taught me what it meant to be a father;
Logan, my Taylor,
who taught me what it meant to be a grandfather;
and the Hemlock girl athletics,
who kept me going when I couldn't see a reason for it.

I AM NOT SURE WHAT WAS causing the sting blurring my vision. The raindrops continued to find their way down through the trees, and running directly into the downfall only added to the force of their fall. But on the other hand, rushing half blinded through the dark made it very hard to avoid head-hanging brush and limbs. I had already been face-slapped more during tonight's run than in all of my teen dating life, and back then I had quite a smart mouth on me.

Still did.

But I couldn't stop. As long as there was the whimper to guide me, it would take more than a little rain, or a few branches to slow me down. Even without the whimper, I was going to keep crashing forward.

I half ducked the next low-hanging branch and once again tighten my grip on the heavy handle in my right hand. I had plucked the ax from a stump at the start of this chase, surprised at how it had come loose without slowing me down, and felt strangely natural in my hand. From the weight of it, I figured the ax would be a damaging weapon.

And I wanted a damaging weapon, because when I caught up with the whimpering, somebody was going to get damaged.

Chapter 1

JOHN'S PHONE CALL SHOCKED ME back to a reality I had finally learned to avoid. It was not easy, but for the most part, I hid it behind replacement memories I could control. My friends got me involve with the local kids attending their sporting events helping with athletic weaknesses, sharing growing-up advice as if I knew what I was talking about, and just being there for them. It had become a half-serious joke about them being my adopted brood.

I gave them attention, and they helped me cope with the end of my world.

Without them?

I might have gone on breathing, but it wouldn't have been living.

And then John called.

John was one of the few people able to rip off my imposed covering of the past to bring the memories back. Not just the facts I could have reburied, but the raw emotions I had never really discarded.

John was too much a part of those memories.

For fourteen months, John had served with Junior in that desert hellhole overseas. They had moved past the word *friends* to become squad mates and brothers in arms. Or as Junior expressed it, "After hearing a couple of bullets zing by, you became very close to those covering your back."

The boys of Junior's unit were great at covering each other's backs, but even they had their limits. After a tour and most of a three-month extension, their luck dealing with roadside bombs took a night off. All the men riding with Junior were injured, with half paying the supreme price.

Junior was among the wrong half.

Riding in the second vehicle, John had been one of the first on the scene. He helped to lift my son out of the twisted metal and then later into the aid station. Watching the medic shake his head over Junior had scared John in a way only a veteran of military conflict could ever understand.

That moment kept us close.

Like most of the soldiers involved in that night, John suffered from survival guilt. Now there was a feeling I could understand. A parent is not supposed to bury their child. Especially an only son. My twin daughters could give me grandchildren, but only a son can carry on the family name.

A dream I never harbored until it sank away.

It took a long time, but like a survivor of the *Titanic*, I had to go on with my life. I dismissed Junior's muttered worries about the possibility of unplanned fatherhood with a girl among the support troops and quit digging after my unlikely hopes. If there was a child, the trail had been ground away in the sands of the Middle East, and even if I found the boy, I had no real legal rights.

Then I got John's call.

"Junior's girlfriend got a hold of me through the grapevine and wants you to meet Taylor."

"Taylor?"

"Junior's child!"

I lowered myself to the edge of the couch and tried to wrap my head around the development. For over a year, I had questioned Junior's comrades about the girl. I even tried checking with anyone in the military who might lead me to a connection.

I got a possible name from a couple of Junior's stateside friends, but it did not lead to anything. She couldn't be found, and my obsession with the search was ripping out my daughter's heart. She felt like she was losing her dad, as well as her brother. Finally, I gave up the search and concentrated on my adoptive brood.

After all, they had given me back my life and a reason for living. And now?

Chapter 2

I WAS STILL MULLING OVER THE question as I dropped my tail on to a fossilized oak bench three weeks later. I have noted this hardness as a common occurrence with airport furniture. I think it comes from the people who use the seats and benches. They are all in a hurry and too busy to relax, so why make the seating comfortable?

Not that it mattered.

I had not been comfortable with anything for three weeks.

I was falling back to the days after my son's death where I existed in a coma between dead to the world numbness and blinding pain. I couldn't even really grieve my loss. Instead, I had to comfort people and tell them how it was okay that my son was blown in half.

"Junior was doing what he wanted to do."

Yeah, that made it all better. So why did I choke up every time I uttered the line and want to cry when some stupid character died on television?

It had taken forever to go through the long list of people that had missed Junior's death. Many had not connected a soldier's face on the television to the memory of a happy-go-lucky kid with a grin for everyone. You could add in a few more, people who had dodged the orbit of my life since the incident. They needed a sign that I was okay so they could feel better about their own lives. Then when I had finally cleared the daily hurtle of comforting others, John's call had crashed into my life.

To change the direction of my thinking, I looked down toward the gate where John would be debarking. Not that I really had to look. With a six-foot-four height and army-hard frame, it was next to impossible not to see John coming.

He would come strolling down the carpet like a lion among sheep.

Junior had the same quality. Not when leaving for basic, but for sure when he returned. If anything he had become a better man than me. In some ways, I had lost my little boy to the army, but in another I had gained a friend.

We talked all the time, first by phone and then by online chat after his deployment. I began looking forward to the future and even liked the idea of being a grandfather. I was going to spoil his kids rotten and teach them every trick Junior had used to drive me crazy. In fact, I had planned several new twists to Junior's tricks. I was going to help him raise the best kids in the world.

Or so I thought, until I received a visit from a pair of unhappy army messengers. They were so uncomfortable that I ended up comforting them. At that moment, I gave up on life and realized how bad a father I had been.

I had changed my mind a million times about this trip. I had even dialed John a few dozen times to cancel and then hung up before the ringing could begin. Twice I had allowed John to answer the phone and then fumbled through some excuses, which did not even make sense to me, let alone John.

Still in the end, I ended up here in the airport, grasping at a connection to a lost future.

Chapter 3

AND JOHN?

He followed through with the loyalty of a brother in arms.

After contacting me, he arranged leave and offered to join me. At first, I begged off, not wanting to drag John in any deeper. John believed different. He figured I might use his absence as a reason to forego the trip.

John even took over the driving, although my Ranger was not the best fit for him. He was tall and stocky while I was short and plump. It only took a few miles to tell he would rather have been in a full-sized Ford 150, but life seldom gives us what we want.

Our conversation went from hot to cold, with the mood of the subject matter. Running on about sports and hunting, John carried the lead about the military and guns, and when our present trip was mentioned?

The talk went frigid.

It's not that I did not have questions.

You could have written a novel based on my questions with enough material left over for a sequel. But the answers scared me to death, and John didn't push the subject matter. It wasn't one of his areas of expertise, and John preferred to keep things simple.

For his age, John was a very smart man.

We were covering the pros and cons of military firearms being used as deer-hunting weapons when we twisted around a mountain slope on a paved road one step above gravel. And there it was, our destination, a postcard-picture-perfect little town.

The town was laid out in Historical East fashion with a clean white church steeple standing guard over the village green. A set of ageless shade trees were stationed around a golf-green lawn with a wooden railed bandstand in the middle. It could have been brought here straight out of *The Music Man*. All it needed for the transition was ninety-six trombones and a band leader.

The buildings surrounding the circle were small shops. I could almost identify the small-town drugstore with a soda jerks counter sitting next to old-time barbershop with the striped pole. A nice match for Mayberry, but the distance made my observation a guess and not reality.

"Perfect little tourist trap."

I started at John's verbal interruption and jerked my mind back to our objective. "Yeah, perfect."

John pulled off to the side of the road and clicked off the motor. "You sure?"

I opened my mouth to confirm the perfect and hesitated. Was my mind seeing something I missed? Taking in the whole village from ridge to ridge, there was nothing to sound the alarm, but . . .

"You would think a tourist trap would have a better road leading in."

"And a McDonald's or Taco Bell to greet the visitors?"

I nodded at John. "And at least one building or house looking newer than the 1950s"

"Want to back off."

"Yes, but you won't let me."

"Much more of this and I might."

I looked at my young companion and saw from the grip on the steering wheel he was as unsteady as me. But none of it made any real sense, probably too much combat for John and too many late-night vampire movies for me. I should have known better, but a guy has to have some sort of escape.

Or go crazy.

Nothing was said for another few moments, and then John restarted the Ranger, and we began rolling toward our meeting.

Chapter 4

SINCE THERE WAS NO PARKING around the green, we settled for parking behind the structure I had guessed at from the hill. I had more or less called it right, only you needed to switch it around with my drugstore guess.

At least I had been in the right topical area, which did not make me feel any better. I would have loved just one peek of vinyl siding or riding mower, but no such luck.

It twisted something old in my stomach.

Did I really belong here?

It didn't feel like it, but maybe I was suffering from fear of the dark?

"Ready to go out front?"

"Nope," I rolled my neck around in the suddenly stiffening collar and gave John my "you got to be kidding" look.

"You came a long way."

"And I'll finish the trip."

Sure I would. This would be my connection to Junior, and this time I would do a better job. No more overtime to put food on the table, I was a lot better situated now. I still had most of Junior's life insurance money as an emergency fund, and since his departure for the army, my expenses had dropped off considerably.

Soon I could retire and spend even more time with Taylor. I would have him tossing a ball and swinging a bat by the end of the end of the summer. There was no way I would ever miss any of his little league games or high school sports. I would even be there sitting front and center for his concerts or plays, if any of his interests went beyond the playing fields. Nothing was going to stop me from being a good parent this time.

Unless this trip was all a scam.

What if Taylor was not Junior's son?

Or perhaps he was Junior's son, but all they wanted from me was money?

"John." I swallow at the watermelon clogging my throat and tried not to squeak. "Taylor's mother?"

"Sandy."

"Yeah, Sandy." I ignored John's displeasure and finished my thought, "Does she seem nice?"

"On the phone?" John grinned before adding, "Very."

"In person?"

"Well, she did choose Junior, but being in Iraq at the time, Sandy didn't have much of a selection." John cupped a hand over my shoulder and twisted me to face him. "In Iraq, Sandy spent most of her time being sad, but when she was with Junior, she smiled."

"Junior had that effect on people."

"Tell me about it." John's eyes held a film of moisture one emotion away from tear. "Junior was one of the best."

"Come on, big fellow." I waved for John to follow me as I headed toward the green and my grandson. It took only two strides for John to match my start and fall in besides me. Another twelve steps, and we were into the green.

And then it happened.

Chapter 5

THE THIRD STORE AWAY FROM the drugstore side of the street was an ice-cream parlor. It had a half-dozen circular tables scattered out front with old chairs, which might have been popular with skinny-butted people a century ago. Their backs and frames were black and wire like with seats of woven fiber.

I preferred cushions.

But Taylor apparently didn't.

Yes, Taylor and I knew the child carried Junior's genes instantly as our eyes meant.

Stranger yet Taylor knew. There was a connection, a family thing of shared blood, genes, or whatever.

Taylor gravitated from the chair and literally bounced across the gap between us. I braced for a chest thud, but it never came. Taylor slammed to a halt just out of grab range.

"Are you my granpa?"

I nodded to confirm and answer with a half question of my own, "You're a girl?"

"Of course." Taylor threw a hand on to her hip, and took a measure of my looks. "You're real old."

"That I am." I held up a hand to forestall Sandy's rebut and knelt down on one knee. "Is that bad?"

Again, Taylor took a study of me, and I of her.

Taylor was small but not undersized. Her body was more like a compaction of supercharged energy, ready to flash out as burst of action.

I could see it in her eyes.

They were a twined set of Junior's. They had his blaze of blue jewel, with golden flecks of Irish luck speckling through them. It was almost ghostlike watching their depths turning over the moment like a mystery waiting to be solved.

The big difference was the hair. Instead of an unruly mop of dark brown, Taylor's face was framed by a floating mass of blond.

No, not blond.

Yellow.

It was like spun silk the color of a yellow rose. So fine that even combed in place several strands drifted in the wind to section Taylor's face with lines of gold. As I watched, a couple caught on her lips and brought about a brush-off by the little lady.

"No, my mommy is old, and I love her."

My glance over Taylor's head caught Sandy's eye roll and John's grin. He seemed to be enjoying the situation. But I was not sure whether it was from my lack of comfort or Taylor's five-year-old cuteness.

Either way, I was on the spot. I knew the cuteness was real, but what if the motive was not? Sandy would not be the first woman to use her child for personal gain.

"Excuse me!"

That snapped my mind back where it belonged.

Taylor's tone brooked no put off from me. She had been brought up right enough to be polite, but still had a five-year-old's sense of self, where the world revolved around her needs.

I wish I could feel the same, but . . .

I brought my gaze back to Miss Taylor and gave her my complete attention. Still she took a moment to put on her most serious face, swallowing twice to clear her throat for the words to come.

"Can I call you Granpa?"

"That would probably work better than *mister* or *hey you*."

And more natural, considering at one time the twins and Junior had all used that same slightly off way of saying grandpa to my father. It was almost like Taylor was carrying on a family tradition.

Taylor nodded like a dashboard bubblehead doll on an unpaved back road; I almost expected it to pop off at the neck and fly into my face.

"Granpa?"

"Yes?"

"Can I hug you?" Taylor's face held the smile, but her eyes were pleading. "I have never been hugged by a granpa."

I opened my arms and got slammed in the chest by a thirty-five-pound crash of energy. It was like an electric current shocking me back to life, providing the one something I had been missing without realizing it.

I folded my arms around Taylor and drank in the warmth of a human body caring without question. It stretched the moment out into a lifetime but ended all too quick when Taylor's patience with confinement ran out. She wiggled back and met my eyes again.

"Can I love you, Granpa?"

Chapter 6

WITHOUT REALLY ANSWERING, I GOT Taylor up and over to the table she had been sharing with her mother. This is where I got my first good look at my granddaughter's mother, Sandy.

She had some extra pounds, but nothing compared to most of my son's choices. They, including his widow, had all been large. Not tall, large. While Sandy had no jiggle, just solid baby fat, probably a leftover present from nine months of carrying Taylor.

Sandy's hair was a match for her name. Very clean, as if it were a common state and not a "let's impress the money" condition. It could have used a perm or cut, but raising a kid as a single parent did a lot to prevent such taken-for-granted extras being a part of life.

Sandy's eyes were a hazel, lovely, inviting, but definitely not the direct source of Taylor's blue eyes. They were dominated by Junior's genes, but the light complexion and hair color came from her mother.

I glanced over at the next table to Taylor's attack on the ice cream she had coaxed out of Granpa and took another measure of the child. Taylor was neat, clean, and well behaved.

That was Sandy doing.

"I didn't think you would come."

"John told you I was coming."

"After our last talk, I think John had his doubts, and I have had my disappointments."

I started to snap off a "That's life" but then thought better of it. I had gathered my own share of disappointments, including one shared with this girl. Like it or not, Junior had promised us both a future with him in it, and neither of us got it.

"I hope she isn't one of them." I nodded toward Taylor, who was in the process of telling John the proper way to eat ice cream. "Your daughter is something special, and she has you to thank for that."

"She deserves more." Sandy brushed at her jeans, which were clean, but the blue denim was worn white in several spots. "Like pretty clothes and dance lessons. Things the other girls have."

"Girls with two parents?"

"Parents with jobs."

"You don't work?"

"I've been laid off." Sandy's back straightened, and her hands moved off the table to rest on the knees. "And my ex would rather leave the country than spend a dime on Taylor."

"Nice guy!"

"A control freak, if he had been a halfway nice guy, I wouldn't have been sleeping with your son."

"Are you sure?" I slid back in my seat and let the bile out. "Junior was a good-looking kid."

Sandy's hazel eyes darkened toward thunderstorm black.

"Not with a bald head, but it didn't matter." She paused for the right words. "He made me feel important."

Sandy words brought my memories to the surface and the iron out of my back. I had seen that before with nieces, nephews, and younger kids. It came from Junior's belief in people, one I used to share.

"This is why I did not contact you earlier."

"Because you cheated on your husband?"

"Yeah, I'm a cheap slut."

"If you say so."

I watched the tears roll down Sandy's cheeks and was not surprised to find a blond hair urchin at her side. Ice cream forgotten and with a tenderness born of Junior's genes, Taylor tried to wipe away the tears and comfort her mother.

I don't know how I reached Sandy's side or got my hand on her shoulders, but it happened. And the words I uttered didn't feel like mine, but they were.

"You were not a cheap anything." I loosened my grip to pat the shoulder. "Young, scared, and very far away from home, but not cheap."

"But I was married."

"And so was Junior." I saw Sandy's chin come up just an inch. "Junior's was a mistake that should have never happened. From what I am gathering, yours was no better."

John from the other side nodded, either with agreement on the marriages or my action. I was not sure which and not sure how much I cared. Sandy wiped away her tears with a napkin and hugged Taylor to her, cooing out a comfort I know she didn't feel.

After a long trio of minutes, she tugged Taylor back a foot and studied her daughter's concerned face. She forced out a crooked smile that had less joy than a hangover on New Year's and wiped at a spot of ice cream halfway to the hairline on Taylor's cheek.

"Looks like one of us needs to wash our face."

"I can wipe it off." Taylor went into face-wiping modes with both hands, doing more moving around than removable.

"I see." Sandy went mock serious and put a finger next to her nose. "But I think our new friend John needs his face washed."

"He's big." Taylor looked back and up at John. "He should be able to wash himself."

"But he doesn't know where the restrooms are. Don't you think you should show him?" Taylor made a face that showed she didn't, but Sandy had a trump card. "He did buy you ice cream."

Well, I was the one who brought the ice cream, but the ploy was working, so I stayed quiet. Taylor on the other hand had no such inclination. She let me have it over the shoulder even as she gathered in John's hand.

"Granpa! Don't you make my mother cry again!"

When Taylor disappeared into the parlor, Sandy turned her attention back to me.

"When I came back from Iraq pregnant, my ex-husband beat the crap out of me and left to go drinking with his buddies." Sandy rubbed at her cheek as if reliving an old pain. "That finished any spark I had left in our marriage. I moved out and filed for divorce the next day."

And then she came after me for money six years later.

I had to wonder.

If there hadn't been a divorce, would I have ever met Taylor?

Of course on the bright side, I could have went on dreaming of a grandson instead of just another granddaughter who would never carry on the family name.

Chapter 7

WE TALKED FOR A WHILE longer, picking each other's brains.

I found out unemployment runs out, and rather than go on welfare, some people fight to stay independent. Sandy was one of those people.

She had hung on for months, cleaning house, taking part-time jobs, and making every penny stretch into a dime. But in the end, the needs of rent did her in. Sandy was on the edge of being evicted when a gentleman from the local church where Sandy was getting free child care offered a solution.

He owned a house a couple hours away in this small town. On the current market, he could not dump it, and maintenance was becoming a drain. If Sandy would take over the lawn care and snow removal, she could live there free.

Sandy did not want to move but was running out of options.

So she started over without friends, and only a one-person family. It wasn't easy, but she picked up enough cleaning jobs to keep them eating three meals a day with a little extra for an occasionally ice cream.

But Sandy felt there was something missing.

Taylor was a bright happy child, who seemed to get along with everyone. But she was asking questions about family and her dad. The truth explained away Sandy's lack of family, but Junior being in heaven only went so far.

Taylor started putting things together and wondered about her real dad's family. Sandy knew about me and Junior's two married sisters. Hiding the fact from Taylor became more difficult by the day.

Until the little slips in Sandy's answers left Taylor a theory her mother could not deny.

The next step was to contact me.

That's where a little research, and John came in. If he had dropped out of the army like many of Junior's squad mates, Sandy may never have found me.

A situation Sandy admitted held plenty of promise.

Sandy fully expected nothing but hate from me. Her own husband had proven that possibility, and I think Sandy, like John and myself, suffered from survivor guilt.

I could understand the feelings but had trouble forgiving them.

Sandy's inaction had cost me a part of Junior that I would never get back.

It didn't help that Taylor was a girl.

I had granddaughters, whom I had held as babies, brought birthday presents, and shared a million hugs. Would it be right for me to give another child a share of their love?

A boy would be easier, having a different place in my heart.

But a girl?

Chapter 8

ICE CREAM ASIDE, WE DECIDED it was time to eat.

I offered to fund dinner, but Sandy would have none of it. She had prepared a dish of lasagna, and while Sandy claimed it wasn't much, John and I both saw the flicker of pride in her eyes.

Not sure about John, but I saw or felt something more.

There was fear in her eyes, the fear of rejection. Whether Sandy was after money or a simple extension of family, she had done her best for Taylor. Being told she was not good enough at anything could be devastating, especially if her little one got caught in the fallout.

I was not going to be the one to give her another kick in the teeth. We ended up eating our dinner at Sandy's.

She was staying in a nice little house on the edge of the village. It basically had two bedrooms and a living room kitchen combo room. The bath held both a shower and tub, with a fair amount of storage for towels and stuff. Other than that, there was only a back shed attachment that held washing and drying equipment but little heat.

Inside I was impressed by the condition the rooms.

The furniture was worn and thread bare in many places, but clean and vacuumed. Having raised a child by myself, I expected toys to be scattered all around the house, but was wrong. There were two Disney DVDs on the coffee table and a collection of coloring books spread across Taylor's bed. The most touching piece of lived-in look was three pieces of dress-up clothes hanging out from under the cover of Taylor's toy chest.

It was an old foot locker from Sandy's army days, and it made me want to cry.

But I didn't.

Instead I watched *Peter Pan* with Taylor while John set the table and Sandy put the finishing touches on the meal. I found out from Taylor that the movie was really about Tinker Bell and that she had the next adventure in her room. Taylor promised to watch it with me later if I explained to her mother how bedtime could be moved back because of my visit.

The moment dropped me back to an earlier day when my kids had tried the same ploy on me; Junior was one of the best.

Tilting her head sideways to look up at me, Taylor broke off a copy of Junior's grin filled with innocent mischief and knowledge. It had taken a lot to resist that smile from Junior and took even more to stay strong with Taylor. But I was not here to cause a disruption in family dynamics.

At least not yet intentionally.

"Your dinner awaits," John made his announcement with a sweeping bow and full-toothed smile.

"I want to sit next to Granpa." Sandy's smile behind John faded. "But, Taylor."

"I would love to eat next to such a beautiful little lady." I found myself beaming a smile equal to the one Taylor reacted with. "And if you don't mind, it might be nice to sit and eat here in front of the TV."

Sandy almost let out a sigh of relief, but it was John who caught on to my reasoning. He rolled his eyes toward the dinette in the kitchen, and I nodded.

It held only three chairs.

I doubt if Sandy expected John or me to stand, and as the hostess, it would be Sandy's duty to claim the third. By my count, such a setting would leave Taylor out.

I returned my attention to the squirming bundle of six-year-old arranging the coffee table. I thought she would make room for herself and maybe me, but I was wrong. With a great amount of childish care, she cleared off space for four places.

All of them were fairly close to being equal. The one closest to me might have been two crayons thicker in width, but was probably wishful thinking on my part.

"And since you, Miss Taylor, have become the hostess, where do I sit?"

"Right here!" Taylor patted the space closest to me. "I made it a little bigger because you are old and might need more room."

Sandy's mouth could not have dropped any further with an anchor attached while John actually dropped to the floor laughing. I fought hard to remain serious, but it became a lost cause when Taylor's eyes went back and forth between her mother and John. My smile became a grin and then dissolved into chuckles and finally full-blown laughter.

About the time I went into the turning-red stage, Taylor's face twisted and crashed. She ran to her mother and clamped on to Sandy's leg, face buried out of my sight.

"Hey, Taylor." I dug back in my memory for the long-forgotten skill of foot removal from mouth. "We're not laughing at you."

That got me a head turn and one-eyed stare.

"We were laughing at me for being old."

"But I don't want them laughing at you."

"Why?"

"Cause you're my granpa." Taylor turned toward me while keeping her arm firmly wrapped around the leg. "And I want to love you."

How do you react to that?

A flippant comment, a half-felt "I love you," or play it semi-serious. Of course while I was checking the choices, Taylor took it out of my hands.

"I never had a granpa before."

Chapter 9

I PUT MY FOOT DOWN WITH Sandy's plan for the sleeping arrangements. Her heart was in the right place, but Sandy wanted to give up her bed and sleep in Taylor's bedroom on the floor. I have been a lot of things in my life, but there are some lines I won't cross. And putting a lady on the floor was one of those lines.

I also put a no-way on John's offer to take Sandy's place on the floor. I could afford a pair of rooms and wanted my privacy. After meeting Taylor, I had a lot of thinking to do.

I mean, first of all, Taylor was not even a boy. He was a she, and I already had granddaughters. How could she fill the hole left by Junior's death?

How could anyone?

I went over that question a few thousands time while trying to sleep at the local Travelers Inn. It kept me awake until long after everyone else quieted down, leaving the parking lot looking like a dimly lit cemetery.

A metaphor I didn't care for but strangely fitting for this community.

I rose early the next morning, but John still beat me down to the breakfast nook. It barely looked big enough for a dozen people when you glance at it from the lobby but had at least twenty tables spread around without anyone feeling crowded.

John had claimed a table to one side, halfway between the entrance and kitchen. He had shifted it around, just enough for both him and me to have our backs more or less to the wall.

John greeted me with a grunt, a menu, and not much else.

His self-imposed quiet suited me.

I still carried around a hangover from last night's thinking.

Studying the menu helped for about thirty seconds, but it contained the same old dishes as every other small-time eatery. If anything, the Travelers Inn made their choices seem even more common and less appetizing.

I settled for a couple of eggs over medium, with rye toast and bacon. I asked for the bacon crispy, but from the bored attitude of the middle-aged woman taking our order, I expected half done and greasy.

Her expression even put off my smart-assed banter reserved for sour-faced waitresses. It came out lame and lifeless and did nothing to bring about a smile. If anything, the expression curdled another degree.

John ignored her cold-shoulder stance and smile as he asked for an army-sized breakfast. His style didn't seem to have any better effect on the woman, and she dotted the order with a sharp stab. She got almost three steps before John's words brought her to a halt.

"And my friend's bacon will be crispy and his eggs soft but not runny. Do you understand?"

The waitress tottered between making a break for the kitchen and answering. It might have gone on for quite a while, but John added another level to the sergeant's voice he used for command.

"Do you understand?"

"Yes."

"Then turn in our orders, please."

She hesitated as if to bark out a "Yes, sir," but instead she nodded and scooted off toward the kitchen at double speed.

"You must be an army noncom."

"Why?" John looked over my shoulder at the owner of the soft purr and smiled. "I could be an officer."

"No, you couldn't." The purr's hand came down upon my shoulder and accidently blocked my head turn. "Your tone of command is earned, not pinned on by an act of congress."

With that observation, I had to see the purr's owner. I forced my chin up and over the hand. Didn't help much. With my chin pushed up, the only thing I could make out was a pale forehead with slivery hair pushed across it. As if reading my mind, the speaker slipped her hand away to reveal a mocking grin of dainty white teeth.

"Is that better, or should I twirl around in front of you like the model on her runway?"

The view was enough, but at the same time far short of what the average man would want. Our purring interruption was a strikingly attractive woman. But I could not tell you why.

The hair was silver, and what I first thought was bottle produced on a closer look might have been natural. It floated around her face like spider silk and was a perfect match for the girl's green eyes and snow-white complexion.

The body?

It had a slender cat-like quality. Probably it was not much over five-six, but the height appeared to be more because of the flow. A grace of ins and outs, which took her small breasts and hips and made them more feminine than any big-breasted woman I had ever met.

Only then did I catch the one imperfection.

Her pupils were slanted up and down instead of round.

"An inherited birth defect."

"Excuse me?"

"My eyes." The girl ran a finger over them to draw a line up and down. "My family all have eyes like this."

Chapter 10

"**M**Y NAME IS SALEM."

The girl slipped behind the chair next to John with a grace both alien and familiar at the same time. But not one I could place.

"Those are my friends, Daniel and Moses." Salem gave an eye point to a pair of guys sitting by the door. "We eat breakfast here once or twice a week."

I could not say much for her choice of friends.

Even from across the room, they gave off a sense of bland. From what I could see, they only had one expression, a frown they could have been sharing. Their dress was almost as identical, consisting of black pants and pale-blue work shirts. Only the shades were slightly different.

"And you three are the local welcome wagon?"

John's question brought out a smile.

"Do I look like the welcome-wagon type?" Salem then gave a peek toward her friends. "Better yet, do they?"

"Not so much." I pushed back a couple of inches to let the waitress set down my orange juice. "But you did come to us."

"Maybe I like tall army men," Her eyes went from John's to mine. "Or short old men who are good with kids."

I took a slow drink of my orange juice, savoring the freshness, which was not there, all the while looking over the rim at Salem.

"You've been watching us."

"Nope, I just noticed you buying ice cream for Taylor."

Chapter 11

JOHN SLIPPED BACK IN HIS chair and measured the girl a second time. After a second, he offered her the empty place, sitting across from me. In reply, Salem shook her head but made no move to leave.

"You know my . . ." I hesitated over the last word and commitment, but forced it out for lack of a better term. "Granddaughter?"

"Sandy uses our child-care organization when working." Salem trailed her fingers over the empty chair. "Father's church provides the service free of charge."

"A preacher's daughter?"

John's interest perked up like a child in a candy shop. From experience, I knew John didn't miss much, but he seldom showed his interest. It was an old army tool he used to supervise without being noticed by the underling. But this girl was quick.

She picked up on the interest even before me.

Salem flicked the tip of her tongue out and twitched the hips with a deliberate familiar beat. The following answer might have been simple, but the words were carefully chosen.

"Father is more of a church leader than preacher." Salem's eyes locked on ours and communicated their attention toward her companions. "He is a parent to none but prefers the title father over his real name."

"Sounds like an interesting guy."

"In many ways." Salem's eyes gave away nothing but her ability to hold a stare. I was beginning to believe this girl was above blinking.

"And Sandy takes Taylor to his church."

"Just the child care." The tip of Salem's tongue showed for a split second. "Sandy is not really Father's type of worshiper."

"He has a type?"

Our strange young lady tilted her head to one side and turned all attention to John and his question. "Doesn't every church?"

"Mine doesn't."

"That would be interesting"—Salem's eyes switched back to me—"and very different from Father's."

"Should I check out this church?"

"Not your type neither." Salem pushed in the chair and waved to her friends. "Their type."

I tried studying Salem's companions without appearing to stare, and it didn't take long. My longer look only confirmed my first impression.

I watched our waitress take their order. They gave orders without either ever changing his frown. They could just as well have been talking marionettes without strings.

"Filling the pews with that type must make for a really exciting service."

"You would be surprised." Salem smiled over her shoulder at the waiting table. "There is more there than meets the eye. And now back to the real issue, what is your interest in our Miss Taylor?"

"Granddaughter!"

"Sandy's parents are dead."

"I'm from the father's side."

Salem gave me the look, daring me to say more.

"Biological father." I met her dare and trumped it. "My son was a man. He would never have walked away from a child in need, his or otherwise."

"Sure!"

Salem again looked to her friends and began to move off, going five full steps before looking back to us. Pausing, more for effect than need.

"And you plan on taking his place?"

"I plan on getting to know my granddaughter."

"And nothing else?"

I nodded the slightest bit, perhaps in yes, perhaps in challenge. To tell the truth, at that moment, I was not sure.

"Best to keep it so." All hint of friendliness left Salem's eyes. "Raising a child of Taylor's age would be extremely hard for someone of your advanced age."

"He'll have help."

Salem got a "cat playing with a mouse" look in her eyes and grinned at John. "Not from you, you'll be deployed."

John's mouth worked without retort as Salem crossed the room and, without the use of words, placed money on the table and left. Her two friends got up and followed without ever being served.

"They didn't eat."

"I don't think Salem or her friends came here to eat."

Chapter 12

UNLIKE SALEM AND HER FRIENDS, John and I did eat. Wasn't the best breakfast I have ever eaten, but with enough salt, the eggs were passable, and thanks to John, the bacon was crisp. By not thinking about the taste, I was able to fill my stomach and concentrate on my conversation with Salem.

She hadn't exactly welcomed us, but maybe it was concern for Taylor and her mother. From what I had found out so far, Sandy had received very little help from her ex-husband or our government.

True, Sandy and Junior had broken the rules by conceiving a baby while deployed, especially since they were both married to others. But in my mind, they deserved a little slack. Both had put their lives on the line for our country, and in the end, Junior had given his.

That should have counted for something.

Yet at the same time, I was not rushing forward to fill the void.

I had dreamed of Junior, holding my grandson and passing our name down another generation. That was not going to happen now. Even if Sandy had shared Junior's name with Taylor, she would eventually be giving it away in marriage.

"Ready to go?"

My mind jerked back to the present as John shoveled in a last bite of a syrup-soaked pancake. The night before, John had questioned the choice of eating breakfast before returning to Sandy's, but she begged off an early arrival. Sandy wanted time to get Taylor up and ready for the day. Sandy stressed that being ready included a visitor-free breakfast for Taylor.

I couldn't blame Sandy.

Last night, Taylor had barely touched her food, preferring to point out things to me. By the time of our departure, John and I had heard the story behind each of her toys and most of the furniture; Taylor was still bouncing off the wall when we made our departure. I counted at least a dozen goodbye hugs between me and John, and there might have been more.

"Do you think Sandy has had enough time?"

"Judging from Taylor's energy level last night, she probably never got to sleep."

"Or Taylor was snoring two minutes after we were out the door."

"The way she was bouncing around." John frowned. "You got to be kidding."

"I'm not. Taylor is going on six, and at that age, nervous energy melts away like snow on a stove." I took a last sip at my orange-colored juice. "Besides, I raised her father, and he was the same way."

John dropped his head and studied his plate as if looking for more food to appear. It didn't. But John's head stayed down as he murmured an observation toward the air between us.

"I never thought of Junior as being little. He was always just one of the guys I trusted to be there."

I tried to think of something to say, but what was there? Junior was one of the guys I trusted to always be there as well.

"We talked about home and family, but the talk only went back so far." I watched a tear roll down his cheek and drop on the plate. "I should have asked more, but I didn't expect him to die."

I watched a few more tears fall before pushing back my chair. Survivor guilt is a hard thing to live with and never quite goes away. I know, I was having trouble fighting back my own tears.

Chapter 13

I T WAS NOT MUCH OF a walk over to Sandy's house, but I drove anyway.

Not out of laziness.

The walk would have probably been good for us, but I was not leaving my Ranger in the inn's parking lot. This town was just a little too strange for my liking, and I wanted my escape out of here within easy reach.

John tapped his window as we cornered on to Sandy's street.

"Daniel or Moses?"

I slowed my turn to make a full study of the young man guarding the corner phone pole. He was dressed in the same bland style as the others, but his hair was lighter with slightly less care taken. I figured it must have been approaching his time for a trim.

"Neither."

"Good, then should I call him Adam or Isaac?"

"Bible names?"

"Fits the others."

"So does Richard and William." Truth as the average person would see it, but the itch behind my right ear wondered if John wasn't right. "And, Salem!"

"Perhaps a slight variation with a hidden meaning."

"Or the person holding Taylor on Sandy's porch."

John's eyes snapped forward, and his hand snaked to the door handle. I think he might have leaped right out of the still-moving truck, except for the grab of my hand. I didn't find a hold, but the touch of my hand was enough to stop him.

Or at least it was until I brought my Ranger to a stop in front of the house. Then I found John clearing the front of my truck before I could get it out of gear or make a move to turn off the motor.

Finally, with the Ranger parked, I cracked the door enough to bring on my dome light and take in the scene. It didn't take a genius to know my contributions were not needed. Before John had a chance to open his mouth, Sandy was off the porch and explaining.

"Salem came over to offer her services as a babysitter while you were in town."

"Did you inform Miss Salem visiting Taylor was the main objective of our visit?"

"She did." Salem bounced a dozing Taylor in her arms as she came over to the top step. "But I figured even then you might want some adult time without a sleepy child getting cranky."

"That is very nice of you." I slipped out of the Ranger to finish my comments. "And if we find ourselves needing a babysitter, you'll be the first one we call."

"Are you brushing me off?"

"Never." I forced out a wide smile, which Salem saw right through and gave back in equal strength. I saw the mouth open to begin a comeback, but Taylor put an end to that.

With a scream of "Granpa," Taylor wiggled out of Salem's arms and down the steps. Crossing the grass to the curb side took only another three bounds and leap of faith into my arms.

"Hey, kid, you got to be careful." I caught Taylor under both arms and swung her to one side and then back out into a hug. "What if I would have missed you?"

"Grandpas never miss, and you are my very own granpa."

"Aren't you going to share?"

"Don't want to." Taylor's lip came out a bit, but quickly went back to a smile. "But if I have to, that will be okay too."

"You are so kind."

I held on to my serious adult expression with a lot of effort and a bit of a grin poking at the edges. It would be very easy to spoil this young lady; she was indeed something special.

But the spoiling would have to wait. At the moment, her mother wanted her daughter to change out of pajamas and into play clothes. And while I did not want to hand over my little lady, I understood the need for proper dress in public.

I hustled Taylor off with a pat on the back side and straightened to watch her leave. A familiar tenderness crawled up my spine. One I had lost track of over the last few years, and it felt good. Only I did not have time to enjoy or recall the history of such a feeling.

Salem had made no attempt to come off the porch, and John was giving her the evil eye. A look more of mistrust than dislike, but with John that could be very close to the same thing.

"Taylor likes you."

"Taylor doesn't know me."

"True," Salem came down two of the four steps, "but children her age often have a gift for sensing good and evil."

"And which are you?"

"Both or maybe neither." Salem looked past my ear. "Taylor might see me as a comfort, like a warm blanket or pet."

With her comments done, Salem brushed past my right side, trailing her hand across my thigh. She gave off a low hum and a sense of ownership.

Then Salem was gone, joining her keeper from the corner and one of the two who had been with her in the diner. Together, they walked away and disappeared around the corner.

Chapter 14

O NCE DRESSED, TAYLOR GUIDED US to the nearest playground. I figured it would be a good place to talk some more, but Taylor had other ideas. As we crossed the last street, she grabbed my hand and tugged me toward the nearest swing set. I thought to beg off, and then my mind flashed back.

I saw a younger Junior holding out a football to play catch.

How many time had I begged off, more worried about the dinner I had to prepare. Peanut butter and jelly sandwiches probably would have been just as good in Junior's eyes.

Or later in life when our Saturday night trip to the midnight showing got cancelled because I was too tired to go back out after work. I could have blamed it on being a single parent, but that didn't cut it in the eyes of my son.

To Junior, I must have been the worst father ever.

Taylor's sharp jerk brought my attention back to the here and now.

I found Taylor's face looking up at me. She was smiling, but it was fading away, as if awaiting another disappointment. I knew there was not much holding off the tears with another adult letting her down.

"It's okay, you can go talk to Mommy."

"Naw, I would rather play with you." I went down on one knee to bring myself closer, "You're much cuter."

The smile charged back full force, and now I was the one fighting back tears.

But even misty-eyed, I was able to push a swing with enough force to keep Taylor giggling for all of ten minutes. After that, she allowed me to keep a merry-go-round spinning at a dizzying speed.

It was followed up by a round of water-fountain drinking, with more splashing than refreshing. It was only when we reached the slide section that I refused to follow Taylor's wishes.

I am just too old to go down a slide without breaking my neck.

But I stood by while Taylor showed me the ins and outs of her sliding repertoire. Who knew there were so many ways to sit, lie, or go down headfirst on a piece of smoothed metal. But I drew the line when Taylor suggested a standing-up effort. It was then I took a moment to notice the difference.

Not a single piece of equipment was made of plastic.

Okay, no big deal.

But there were also no modern climbing toys, with trot across bridges and wooded creations for the young climbers to get their early training for the mountains of the future.

In fact, you could have transferred this playground back to my elementary school without anyone noticing the change.

I guess they were in no hurry to change around here.

About then, John stepped past me and grabbed the sliding Taylor mid-giggle. With hardly an effort, he swung her around and up on to his shoulder for a piggyback ride.

"Hey, kid, you and I are making a run to the nearest PX or 7-eleven for refreshments."

"But, Granpa!"

John cupped his mouth as if sharing a secret with Taylor, even thought I would hear it from a yard away.

"He's old and would probably slow us down." Taylor looked from John to me, more than a bit puzzled. "And besides, maybe we can sneak in some candy without the adults around."

Candy did not have to be mentioned a second time to get Taylor's agreement. With a reach-down hug, she grasped the top of my head and told me they would be right back and not to go anywhere.

"Don't worry, I'll stay right here."

Then I laughed as Taylor twisted around a half dozen times to make sure I was keeping my promise. But she did not have to worry. I would have been a fool to leave her, and with Taylor I never want to play the fool in any shape, size, or circumstances.

Chapter 15

"TAYLOR REALLY TOOK A LIKING to you."

"Taylor is a sweet kid and probably has everyone eating out of her hand with the first smile."

"True, but seldom does Taylor return the love."

"Right!"

"No, it's true."

Sandy came up to stand just to my right, watching the same spot as me. The one John and Taylor had disappeared around moments before.

"Taylor has gotten a bit shy since coming here."

"I don't blame her." I felt a shiver of creepy run up my spine with the words. "The people are not the most friendly I have ever met."

"They don't like outsiders."

"Where does that leave you?"

"Tolerated." Sandy kicked at the ground as if looking for a lost quarter. "But just barely. Even the ladies I clean for treat me like a piece of trash."

"Why stay?"

"Taylor has a roof over her head." Sandy's kicks took on a lot more force. "And one thing your son taught me was the kid's welfare always comes first."

"Sounds like Junior."

Sandy stopped her kicking to study my face.

"Do you have any idea how much Junior loved and respected you?"

I chuckle at the thought.

"Do you know what he called me in high school?"

"The monster!" Sandy's face drifted off to a memory shared. "And yet where did he and his friends hang out?"

"I always had plenty of food in the house."

"And an ear to listen."

"Somebody had to."

Sandy reached out to gather in my arm and turn me toward a nearby picnic table. Her next comment did not come until we were turning to sit.

"Even before he found out I was expecting, Junior told me at least a hundred times how he wanted to have several kids." Sandy sucked in the next breath as if clinging to the moment long ago and far away. "Junior told me how he was going to raise them just like his dad."

I sat there for a long minute or two, trying to absorb the information.

I wanted to believe; I needed to believe. If I had been a good father, there would be less reason to go through the dreaded "What could have beens" and more reason to concentrate on the good times.

About then, I realized Sandy had begun speaking again. I shook away the self-imposed fog and asked her to repeat herself.

"Remembering the way Junior talked about you is why I decided to make contact."

"To be a granpa?"

"And more."

It seemed my first doubts had been right. I wanted to ask how much and then leave. But before I get the words out, Sandy went on.

"We have no future here, and Taylor needs a loving home while I get back on my feet."

By the end of first sentence, the tears were coming down like a flowing creek, and the words were becoming garbled. But I had understood worse and understood her all too clearly now.

"I want you to take her home with you."

Chapter 16

OUR CONVERSATION HAD NO CHANCE to go further, because before I could push away my shock, a double-sized soldier came around the nearest corner, doing his best horse trot. The best part of the approach was listening to his giggling rider screaming for him to go faster.

By the time John pulled up next to us, with a pawing of the ground and loud whinny, I was laughing tears. I didn't hear any laugher from my side, but when Sandy stepped up to help our little cowgirl down, she was beaming like a desert sun at high noon.

"Better wait to open those sodas." John handed a plastic bag to Sandy, a match for the one swinging around Taylor's arm. "Or you're going to get a sticky shower."

"Sodas?"

"A pair of Cokes, couple Mountain Dew, some cold water, and a grape soda for the little lady." John tapped his finger in the direction of Taylor's head, trying to hide his words from Sandy. "And maybe a small assortment of candy for later."

"Right." Glancing at the size of the bags, I figured it would last for a lot of laters.

"Pops!"

"If Taylor talked you into anything more, I don't want to know."

"Daniel or one of his brethren is over at the corner, watching us."

Without moving my head, I followed John's head motion with my eyes. It took a moment, but from here, the man standing by the corner looked like one of Salem's goon squad. He had the right outfit, but I could not make out his face from this distance.

"When did you spot him?"

"Didn't." John did a double-check to make sure Taylor was still lining up the bottles at the picnic table she had chosen. "Taylor saw him first."

"She didn't want to say hi?"

"Taylor didn't want anything to do with him." John's face clouded over with a serious look probably reserved for combat. "She jerked me to a stop and begged me to go around the block away from him."

"But she likes Salem."

John shrugged. "Salem is female?"

"That she is." I looked over at my approaching little lady, who apparently had the bottles arranged to her liking. "But I'm not sure Salem's friends are even human."

I shut my mouth before saying anything else and stepped forward with my arms spread. With a garble shout that might have been "Granpa," she jumped into my two-hand grip, and I swung her up on to my back. Probably not with the grace of John, but after a little shuffling, I got the job done.

"Do you want to leave?" Sandy greeted me without a smile.

"Why?"

"Taylor told me about Father's man."

"Do you think he's dangerous?"

"They scare me at times." Then Sandy's smile peeked back out. "But not with you and John around."

"Mostly John?"

"Mostly you." Sandy reached out to take the listening Taylor down from my shoulders. "Junior told me you had a strength about you that always made him feel safe."

"He did?"

"Yes," With Taylor still in her arms, Sandy leaned forward to hug me. "And now I understand why."

Yeah, I thought to myself.

You're both crazy.

Chapter 17

WE CHATTED FOR A BIT longer while Taylor finished about a third of her drink and none of the candy. Then with an excited "Let's go," Taylor was off and running. She got all the way to the swing set before turning back to yell a second time.

"Come on, Granpa. We have to play."

So we played.

We played until it was time to eat. That is when I spoke without thinking.

"Where do you want to eat, Taylor?"

"McDonald's!"

"Sounds good to me." At least better than a lot of places Taylor could have chosen. Father's watcher had ruined my mood for screaming munchkins or grumpy wait staff.

But Taylor wanted more than an okay from me.

"You promise."

"Sure."

"Cross your heart."

"Not sure I have one."

"Granpa!"

"Okay." I held up both hands to stall off the rising temper. "I promise, cross my heart and all."

Too bad Sandy put an end to the Mickey D idea.

She did not have a car, and the nearest McDonald's was located in the next city over. In fact, there were no fast food places in town. Just a few diners and restaurants staffed by people I did not want to order food from.

The only good thing about the situation was my granddaughter's confirmation of the family bloodline.

"But Mommy, Granpa has a car."

"Granpa has a truck," Sandy corrected Taylor, "and there is no room for your car seat."

"There is on the passenger seat."

"And where would John and I sit?"

"John's big, he could sit in the back."

"Taylor!"

Sandy's exclamation would have carried more weight without John breaking into a fit of laughter. It earned him a dirty look from Sandy and a finger pointing from Taylor.

"See!"

"No, I don't." Sandy's look went from dirty to frosty cold. "Listen, young lady, we are not putting John in the back of a truck. And before you suggest it, I'm not sitting in the back."

Taylor glanced to me but swallowed the thought without a word. But then again, she was not done. There were other ploys to try.

"Well, you could stay home."

"Alone?"

"John would stay with you."

"He will not."

"Sure I will."

Well, so much for frosty cold, Sandy's stare switched directions toward blazing hot. And John found himself doing a quick retreat to the far side of table.

"Listen, everybody, we are not going anywhere tonight." A switch of direction by Sandy's glare clapped Taylor's mouth shut. "I will grab something and fix dinner."

"No, you won't. Taylor and I will grab something and fix dinner."

Chapter 18

TAYLOR AND I HIT THE local market to put together our culinary masterpiece. I suggest hot dogs, but Taylor leaned toward fish sticks. We ended up buying both and opting for a multi-choice main course, with a side dish of chips and dip. Even then, the choice took a discussion.

I grabbed a bag of regular chips off the second-to-the-top shelf and plunked them into our shopping cart. I started to push away when I found a hand pushing back on the front of the cart.

"The ones with ridges taste better."

"Do they?"

I got a very serious nod and justification. "It said so on television."

"But I have always…"

Taylor's head cocked to one side. "TV!"

"Take one of each?"

Taylor glanced back at her mother with a frown and quivered her head back and forth.

"I'm paying."

"I don't want to spend all your money and make you sad."

"It will take more than two bags of chips to make me sad."

The words came out sharper than intended. While my granddaughter tried her best to maintain control, she was only six. I watched her features dissolve toward total misery, and I felt an old tightness in my swallow.

"Taylor, I will make you a deal." I went down on one knee to be at Taylor's eye level and then lifted her chin gently with the forefinger of my left hand. "If I spent too much money and get close to being sad, I will tell you so."

Taylor's lip slowed away its trembling, but the moisture in her eyes still hung thick and ready to fall. I could see there was something going on behind the dampness, but nothing I could understand.

"Granpa?"

"Yes?"

"When you tell me, can I help you be less sad?"

Taylor wiped at the tears about to fall with the back of her sleeve and looked at me for an answer. It wasn't one I could give easily. It had been too long since I trusted anyone with such a task.

The eyes in front of me demanded an answer, but not now.

"We'll talk later after our shopping is done and no one else is around."

Taylor's eyes told she was not happy with my answer, but she glanced toward her mother and seemed to understand. Only it was not John or Sandy I was worried about.

It was the pair behind them at the end of the aisle who made me nervous. They were paying too much attention to us, and personally, I was getting tired of seeing Father's puppets every time I looked around.

Chapter 19

FTER CHECKING OUT, WE WALKED back to Sandy's place and found a figure sitting on the top step of the porch. The slender figure had her legs curled underneath from the side and looked more comfortable than any human had a right to be. I knew from the hair color it had to be Salem even before she turned to peek at us over the near shoulder.

I felt a twist in my gut and wanted to kick her tail around the block, but Taylor realized who was waiting at the same time. She rushed forward to give Salem a blow-by-blow description of our day.

It didn't lessen my anger, but watching Taylor's arm-flying demonstration of our day took the air out of it. The best I could do was work on a hard grimace and go forward with the adults.

"Didn't expect you to come back today," Sandy greeted her strange taste in friend with the widest smile of the day. "But glad you did."

"Figured you might need some dessert." Salem reached back to pick up a plastic bag stretched out at the bottom in a pie shape and held it toward Taylor. "Like cheesecake with blueberries on top."

Taylor squealed and reached for the offered bag only turning to me when the prize was firmly in her grasp.

"Can Salem eat with us, Granpa? I'll share mine with her, if we don't have enough."

"We have enough."

Only Salem noticed I didn't say yes, and she gave me a smile saying so.

The smile grated my nerves like a rough piece of sandpaper. At that moment, I would have given up the use of my middle finger for a chance to jerk Salem up to slap the smile off her face.

Still, this was Sandy's house.

"More than enough," I quipped a second time and added a jab for good measure, "especially now that we have dessert."

Sandy stepped over to take my arm and led me into the house. John brought up the rear, taking his time to check out the corners in front and behind us. When he came through the door, his eyes met mine, and he nodded.

"Any chance your friends will try to join us."

"Members, not friends."

"Church of Our Father?"

"Close." Salem helped Taylor slide the plastic bag into the depths of the refrigerator. "They call it the C of Our Father."

"Doesn't the *C* stand for church?"

"I image so." Salem ran her hand over the top of Taylor's head as she closed the door. "But I never really thought about it."

I gave Salem a long once-over. It was almost like she was trying to tell me something, but I didn't know the right questions. Or perhaps Salem was just pulling the chain to get a rise out of me.

"You're trying to tell me you do not know the name of your own church?"

"Not a member." Salem leaned over to give Taylor a little tap on the back side as a nudge toward me. "Didn't you tell me you were going to help your Granpa cook?"

"But you can help."

Salem leaned over to Taylor and staged whisper into her ear.

"There are some things that shouldn't be shared." Salem's head tilted so her eyes could meet mine. "Like this moment with your Granpa or membership in a sect of all males."

Before Taylor could ask what a sect was, Salem rose to join John and Sandy in the other room. She nestled her way into another feet curled under position next to John.

From there, our eyes could meet, but private conversation even in half riddles was nearly impossible. Especially with a pair of young hands tugging at me for cooking help.

Chapter 20

I FIGURED THAT WAS THE END of any adult conversation for the night. At least until Taylor went into a knee-crossing squirm I knew all too well from my earlier child-rearing days.

I also knew the results.

"Taylor, why don't you go wash your hands in the bathroom?" I saw both relief and worry in her eyes, so I added, "I'll wait for you to come back before starting."

"You will?"

"Yep, no matter how long it takes." I patted Taylor's tail to send her off. "Just in case you have to do more than wash your hands."

I straighten up and figured I had a couple of minutes with the adults, but of course, I was wrong.

Before I could make a move to join the others, Sandy noticed Taylor's departure and came out to talk to me. She was not my first choice of conversation. Then again, there was a subject I needed to go over with the lady, so Sandy was better than nothing.

"I didn't finish."

"I was hoping as much."

Sandy leaned against the counter and fidgeted with a dish cloth. I didn't want to hurry her, but Taylor would be coming back all too soon. I guess Sandy realized the same thing, because before I could nudge the conversation forward, she spoke.

"When I said I wanted to send Taylor home with you, I did not mean forever."

I didn't know whether to sigh in relieve or disappointment. But believe me I sighed, and Sandy took it as a sign. Not sure of what, but it pushed her into talking faster.

"I just need to get out of this town and back on my feet." Sandy's next twist of the dish cloth was accompanied by a ripping sound. "About the only things I own here are our clothes and a few of Taylor's toys. I don't want to raise Taylor in a shelter, and I don't have anyone else I can trust."

"And you trust me?"

"Junior did!"

"He didn't know any better, I was the only parent he had."

"Junior knew perhaps better than his father." Sandy dropped the tattered cloth and reached out to take my arm. "And I've seen how Taylor trusts you."

"Taylor likes everyone."

"She doesn't like Father's people." Sandy's grip tightened. "Or most men for that matter."

I am not sure what that said about my masculinity, but it gave me something to think about, which is what I was going to have to do, because my hand-wiping helper came rushing back with the bath towel still in her hands.

"Are you ready, Granpa?"

"Yes, I am."

Just not quite sure for what.

Chapter 21

DINNER WENT FAIRLY WELL. JOHN and I stayed away from the fish sticks, but Taylor and Salem made up for our disinterest. They dug into the sticks like they were fresh-caught trout.

They were both into their second round when I noticed the strange way they were eating the sticks. Instead of wolfing them down straight off the plate, they were picking them up and using their fingers to strip off the breading.

Taylor was still putting both the fish and breading into her mouth, but Salem was not. She nibbled at the fish while pushing the breading off to one side of her plate. From what I could see, the breading was not being saved for dessert.

"Taylor, where did you learn how to eat fish sticks?"

"Salem taught me." Taylor grinned like the Cheshire Cat from *Alice in Wonderland.* "They taste better this way."

I let my eyes drift to Salem.

Those strange eyes of Salem's met my challenge with one of her own. She broke off a morsel of the stripped stick and nibbled it down in three tiny bits. Then Salem licked at her fingers to gather off any missed fish.

"I prefer my fish untainted."

"Surprised you don't like them raw."

John's comment showed how close the others were watching our mostly silence exchange.

"I do." Salem tilted her head slowly to see John. "But sushi is hard to find in our town."

"Then maybe you should move to a big city."

"I wish I could." Salem's stare remained blink-less, but the muscles to either side of her mouth did do a tiny twitch. "But unfortunately, I have attachments here."

"Me?"

"Mostly but not entirely." Salem gave forth her first real smile of heartfelt emotion, and I guess I was not surprised to see it aimed at my granddaughter. Taylor seemed to bring the best out of everyone, even Salem.

"The father?"

"He has been important in my life."

The smile remained, but it lost the glow and became less human. It made me wonder if I had not seen it before somewhere in my life. But before I could question my thought, the topic turned again to McDonald's.

"Interesting menu, but I bet your first choice was McDonald's."

"Taylor?"

My granddaughter froze with her next bite an inch from being consumed. Taylor's eyes darted from Sandy to Salem with the terror of true confusion. I could almost hear the "Not me!" screaming in Taylor's mind and expression.

"She didn't say anything." Salem held out a hand toward Sandy and then turned it over to take the blame, "But I know my Taylor. She would rather eat at McDonald's than any place else."

My Taylor was much softer than Sandy's.

"I like McDonald's, but the fish sticks are good."

"Looks like I need to rent a car for tomorrow."

Taylor wanted to smile but stiffed it as she watched Sandy's discomfort out of the corner of her eye. I was ready to exhibit my status as elder when Salem beat me to it.

"No need to rent a car." Salem stared directly at Sandy. "Father told me to offer you one of his."

"He has already done so much."

"And he wants to do more." Salem pushed the last of her stripped-down stick into her mouth and added, "Father had a big interest in you, Sandy."

The comment would not have bothered me as much, but as the words came out, Salem shifted her complete attention to Taylor.

Like a predator sizing up its prey.

Chapter 22

I DID NOT GET ANOTHER REAL chance to talk with either Sandy or Salem.

If I had, I am not sure what I would have said. I felt like this whole thing was slipping over my head, and it was about time for me to head back home.

Back where my old life waited for me, with no worries or choices I did not want to make. Just an easy day-by-day existence with my friends, daughters, and granddaughters. That all sounded great to me except for one thing.

There would be no Taylor.

Not the end of the world.

Taylor was not the grandson I had been looking for to continue our family name. In fact, she was legally someone else's problem, but . . .

I could see Junior in Taylor's smile. Maybe not in the "I love the world" one she showed most of the time. But in the one you caught when she was measuring you out of the corner of her eye and telling herself she had a secret. Usually it was a secret leading to mischief.

I really missed that look.

And I missed having Junior to talk to.

Junior was the one person I could talk to with no emotion or subject off limits.

I could have tried talking to John, but he was back at Sandy's. John and I both had misgivings about being followed by Father's followers. Sandy assured us it was nothing to be worried about, but we overruled her objection and forced her to accept John sleeping on the couch.

The disturbing part was the lack of an objection from Salem. She remained on the floor, playing Barbie to Taylor's administrations. If anything, she went out of her way to ignore our conversation, only coming alive after Taylor had fallen asleep.

Then it was just a quick goodnight kiss to the forehead of our sleeping little one and out the door. I followed a few minutes later with a hesitation on the porch to check the corners for possible lurkers. There were none I could see. Then I took my Ranger back to the Inn and another round of thinking.

When I had left Sandy's, John had already settled in on the couch, feet hanging over the edge. Sandy was headed to her bedroom to change, and Taylor was curled up on the floor near the end of the couch.

She had faded out while kneeling behind Salem brushing out the long silver hair. It looked to be a movement both familiar and loved by both.

The brushing had left Taylor smiling in her sleep.

And Salem had actually hummed like a cat being petted.

I found myself wondering if Taylor had Junior's touch with animals. My best friend had a farm, and it always amazed me how Junior had been able to pick up feral cats as if they were house pets. Personally, I was never able to get within spitting distance of them, and I had yet to see anyone else get close enough to try picking up the cats. Not even when we had offered food in our hands.

The whole thinking thing left me little time for sleep.

I tried using the broadband on my laptop computer but didn't get a sniff of a signal. I figured it must have been the mountains and a local population too bland to demand service.

I gave up and tossed and turned for the rest of the night. It took a full rotation of hot and cold shower water to work off my fatigue the next morning. I didn't think I could handle another breakfast in the cafe down below, so I grabbed some cold fixings and headed to Sandy.

I got there just in time to meet Father.

Chapter 23

I HADN'T PLANNED ON MEETING THE Father. In fact, deep inside, I was probably hoping to avoid him. I was already in further than I had planned. Going another step?

The first sign of a difference were, of course, the watchers.

By now, I was getting good at spotting Salem's pet walkers, and this time, there were four of them. A couple of them were familiar pair from the cafe, and the others were new but dressed in the same out-of-date outfits. Add that to their love of hanging-around corners, and I had a match.

Their upgrade to four was disturbing, and the car parked in front of Sandy's was even more so. The idea of meeting the driver of said car racketed my feelings up and beyond any level of disturbing I had ever imaged.

I thought about turning around and heading back to my room but didn't get a chance. Before I could react, I saw a yellow-haired munchkin tugging at her mother's hand and waving toward me. Right then, I could not think of a single excuse Taylor might accept.

Besides, I am not sure I wanted to try.

Watching Taylor's excitement did a lot toward stiffening my backbone. Little kids have always been a weakness of mine. Very few of them knew how to fake a smile or stab a back; that usually came later in life.

Swallowing my misgivings, I pulled up behind the car and parked.

The car was a Ford Taurus in a lousy choice of colors. It was an orange bronze, gaining popularity with people who wanted to be different, but I figured it was just plain ugly.

I liked the old farm pickup pulling in across the street better. It had more rust spots than an African leopard and mud flaps draped heavily with clumps of dried dirt. It might once have been navy blue, but the side in view had been repaired with a white panel, and the far front fender was red.

The driver's hair was the familiar silver, and I didn't need to see the face or catch her greeting wave to know it was Salem. A good thing, because my attention was dragged away from Salem's arrival by a little arm tugging at the door handle.

I had parked just far enough away from the curb to make it a hard reach for Taylor to get a good grip on my handle. If I tried opening the door, it might knock her over, and she was too excited to listen to me. We might still be there, if John had not picked up the frantic bundle and helped her slip in through my open window.

Because of the distraction, I missed the driver of the Ford, making his dismount. When I looked up, he was already clear of the curb area and laughing at Taylor with Sandy and Salem. It only took one look to realize Father was not the man I had envisioned.

Christopher Lee, Vincent Price, or any other tall creepy villain would have been my first choice of what I had expected. During the night I had run through the images of a large overweight Asian or a wrinkled up little man hating everyone in the world taller than him. Even just an average Joe I could have expected.

But for Father to turn up as a tiny Santa Claus?

Never in a million guesses.

So maybe I was wrong about everything connected with the Father.

Chapter 24

THE OLD MAN STANDING NEXT to the girls was shorter than me by three or four inches, and on a good day, I was lucky to reach the five-six mark. His belly was rounded like a cross between Porky the Pig and Santa Claus, and no doubt it shook like a bowl of jelly when he laughed.

The beard was shorter than Santa's but white and fluffy like a swirling snowfall. A perfect match for the circle of white around the double silver-dollar-sized bald spot gleaming in the sun. The eyes went along with the program, bright blue and twinkling.

And Father was dressed for the event. Reddish slacks with suspender over a gray flannel shirt. The only thing missing to the Saint Nick look was a pipe and red jacket.

And perhaps a better smile.

Father's grin came easy enough as he stepped forward to greet me, but the eyes had no sparkle. It felt more political than genuine, but then again, I think that can be said for many church leaders.

"So this is little Taylor's grandfather."

"That's what Sandy tells me."

"Strange, I thought there would be more of a family resemblance." Father stroked at his beard with thumb and forefinger. "Taylor is so much lighter than you."

"Yep, just like my daughters." I offered a handshake without any real feeling behind it. "It seemed only my son, Junior, cared enough to follow the family coloring."

"He must have been a handsome fellow."

"The girls thought so."

"Just like his father." Salem stepped into the conversation, nudging against the hand at Father's side.

Father glanced down at the hand and seemed to gather in a thought momentarily lost. He turned it over to expose a set of keys and reached out to offer them to me.

"In any case, I heard my little friend, Taylor, wants to go to McDonald's, and your truck is not really made for four."

"Not really, but if I had to, I could make do."

"No need." Father rolled the key chain around in his fingers. "I have several cars sitting around, unused. This one could use a drive through the mountains and a rotation of fresh gas."

"Awful nice of you." I allowed Father to turn his hand over and drop the keys into mine. "But how will I repay you?"

"Just keep my little one and her mother safe from harm."

The addition of *her mother* came after a pause as if uttered in afterthought. But the pause could very well have been my imagination. So far, Father had done little to raise a normal man's doubts, but I have not been normal since the day a young officer and well-worn sergeant had come to visit.

"Shouldn't be too hard." I glanced down at the fingers wrapped around the thumb of my left hand. "I think it is the other parents who should be worried."

"Or guardians?"

I meant the challenge in Father's eyes with one of my own and fired back.

"Sure, they can be included,"

A smart man would have stopped there, but not me. I had to add a little dig.

"Especially those with no real legal claim to their wards."

Father went all Santa on me, letting out a big belly laugh and clapping me on the shoulder like an old friend at the BBQ. The slaps might have been a little heavy-handed, but how bad could they be from a guy so short he had to reach up to deliver the blows.

It left me little to come back with, except as answering smile. I tried to make it a good one, but it had little warmth and was quite weak. Probably left Father the hero in most eyes, but the opinion I cared about was still gripping my thumb.

Taylor had stayed slightly behind, keeping me between her and the Father. I can't claim Taylor's positioning was intentional, but it felt so, and I was not about to make her move.

The conversation continued on for a few more minutes with my part decreasing. By the time Father turned to leave, I had become dead silent. A lot like Taylor and Father's companion, Salem.

Taylor had not spoken since our dismount from my Ranger, and Salem was just about as quiet. Salem had not spoken since her nudge on during the key exchange. Not even when the Father made teasing comments about her driving and how she was only allowed to drive the pickup because there was no way to damage it further.

It didn't seem to be coming across as a tease. Salem never broke a smile, and I thought his choice of words could have been better.

It was only as we walked Father toward the truck across the street that Salem dropped back beside me. She leaned down to give the top of Taylor's head a kiss and hair rub.

The whisper for me was almost missed.

"*Legal* is a term usually defined by those in power, like the Father."

Chapter 25

SALEM'S COMMENT DID LITTLE TO spoil my day.

I did stop by my inn room to grab the laptop, but I might have done that anyway. There was no way I was going to let Father or his lackey ruin my afternoon.

The drive to McDonald's went through the most rugged territory I had ever visited. At times, it cut through gaps where the rock walls to either side were straight up. I am not sure I could have made the twenty to the thirty feet climb to the top climbing gear and a month's training.

The open spaces were even more beautiful.

In most places, the slopes to either side were covered with old growth, some of it going back to a time before us white people had invaded the continent. The rest, while replanted growth, was fast working its way toward the rugged beauty of the old forest. Another time, another place, I might have enjoyed walking among the trees.

But today I had a breakfast to share.

Actually, I spent most of breakfast in the playroom, watching Taylor romp through plastic balls and making a strong effort to wear out the bottom of her jeans coming down a plastic slide. It had been a lifetime since I had taken a moment to watch a child at play. I hadn't realized how much I had missed it.

I even forgot to eat my breakfast.

Not that I missed or needed it.

I was busy making plans for a shopping trip.

Sandy tried to beg off, but I used the grandfather's ploy. How I never got to do anything for my own kids when they were young. So didn't that give me the right to spoil Taylor just a little?

And it would give me a chance to push Sandy a little harder for information.

That chance came when Taylor went screaming off in Toys R Us. I would have chased after her, but John beat me to the punch. Grabbing a shopping cart, he charged down the aisle like a cop car after a speeder.

I might have worried about the other shoppers, but John was laughing like a hyena in heat. Any person not smart enough to get out of the way of such a laugh deserved to be run over.

"Sandy, you mentioned me taking Taylor."

Sandy's joy melted away. "And have you decided?"

"Not yet," I looked away from Sandy, not really wanting to see her reaction. "Wouldn't it be easier for me to lend you some money?"

Sandy's "No!" came out as a whisper but held the fury of a storm. When I braved a look back to Sandy, I found her shaking with tears.

"I grew up living off the system and joined the army to get away from it. But like an addict, I don't trust myself to go back on the charity of others."

"But . . ."

"No buts." Sandy held up both hands to forestall my protest. "It took a lot of pride swallowing to convince myself letting you care for Taylor was okay."

"Because I am her grandfather?"

"Because you are Junior's father."

Slim difference, in my eyes, but maybe not in Sandy's. "And if I don't take Taylor?"

"Father's people will make sure I survive, but there would be no chance of Taylor and me building an independent life."

"You trust the Father?"

"He has been good to us." Sandy hunched her shoulders to ward off an unfelt chill. "He is not the most normal person, and his followers give me the shivers, but what do you expect from an all-male church?"

Something better than a man who kept a creature like Miss Salem around for a pet. There was something very creepy about their relationship. I'm not sure what, but something.

"Father kept us out of the shelters and made sure we had enough to eat." Sandy's hand grabbing my arm ended the thought before I had to time to finish it. "That is more than you or the army ever did for us."

"I tried."

"To what?" Words and tears were flying so hard, I wasn't sure what to do. "Find us and then turn your back on us like Junior."

"Junior."

"Junior died. He got himself killed on a patrol he should have never volunteered for." The fury left Sandy like a burst balloon. "But Junior wanted to do his share. Why couldn't he have let somebody else do it?"

"He didn't mean to die."

"But he did." Other eyes might have held more pain, but I had never seen it. "And Taylor never got a chance to know her father."

Chapter 26

NEITHER OF US HAD MUCH more to say.

I found a bench to sit on while Sandy went off to gather herself in the ladies' room. I didn't blame her. I almost wished I had a place to hide myself.

Several of the clerks and a couple of customers had witnessed our exchange. Most of them gave me the "Are you a wife beater" look with only the one guy at the beginning of the diaper aisle giving me support. He had a trio of little ones, and from the way his wife glared at him, I had probably plenty of reasons to envy the fact I was not the one crying.

It took Sandy the better part of quarter hour to rearrange her face, and then it was only partially repaired. Sandy's eyes were solid pink and puffed up like an amateur boxer who had just gone a couple of rounds with the heavyweight champion of the world.

And from what I could see, Sandy had not been on the winning side.

But then again, there was no way I could claim a victory.

Sandy may have been dragged out emotionally, but the conversation had dragged up a lot of my own feelings. Not the good ones.

Sandy and I sat at opposite ends of the bench, waiting for the two happier ones to return. Neither of us had any energy, and our wait was the quietest half hour in history. I know the length of our wait because I checked the big clock over the door about once every twelve seconds.

When Taylor did come into sight, she bounced rather then walked. You would have thought Taylor had just won the Super Bowl, World Series, and most of the Olympics medals from both the summer and winter games.

John followed behind Taylor with a shopping cart filled to the rim with a selection of toys fit for a small child-care center. I would never have believed one kid could pick out so many toys in such a small time.

"Have you got enough?"

In response, I got a bouncing bundle of energy leaping into my arms.

"Not all mine, not all mine."

"You got a mouse in your pocket I don't know about."

"Nooooo." Taylor gave me the look reserved for old men being silly. "John wanted the squirt guns and some of the stuffed animals."

"You're not a stuffed-animal person?"

Taylor threw her arms out to either side in a "not really" motion.

"I already sleep with an army bear. How many more do I need?" John pushed up the cart as we talked, and Taylor leaned into my arms to whisper in my ear. "But don't tell John. I don't want to hurt his feelings."

The leaning over is what upset the fruit cart. As Taylor finished her whisper, she caught sight of Sandy's face and no longer wanted to be in Granpa's arms.

"Did you hurt my mother?"

Taylor's eyes may have been only a few inches from mine, but their glare put a million miles between us and yet at the same time brought us closer.

It was a copy of Junior's glare when he found out his sister's first boyfriend had dumped her. It had taken a lot of talking from both me and his sister to keep him from heading out to Texas from Michigan by foot if necessary.

Family is important, and Junior had his own definition of family.

Junior had claimed no friends, because as he stated more than once, if a person was close enough to be friend, they were close enough to be considered family. And Junior claimed one hell of a large family.

So I brushed through Sandy's "I'm just tired" and told Taylor the truth.

"I did." The glare ran up a hundred more degrees. "It was not intentional, but I did."

"Intentional?" Taylor's head cocked away from me in question, but the heated glare did not lessen.

"I did not mean to do it."

"Then why did you?"

"I made a mistake, by accident."

Taylor's eyes went from Sandy's face to mine three times. Each time, putting me under an examination that would have made a Catholic nun proud and thankfully allowing a little heat to evaporate away.

"Don't do it again."

Taylor's eyes were still smoldering, but I felt forgiven. Not that I was smart enough to leave it there, I felt I had to be honest.

"I will try not to, but I'm not perfect. I make mistakes."

Taylor wiggled out of my arms and went over to her mother.

Chapter 27

FROM THERE, OUR SHOPPING WENT down the drain. Taylor refused to accept any of the toys and told John to put them back. I did my best to overthrow the idea, but Taylor carried another character trait passed down by her father.

Taylor was as bullheaded as her grandfather.

The more I insisted we purchase some of the toys, Taylor dug in and told me I should spent the money on her mother. Taylor had toys; her mother had nothing. Not exactly true, but when had a six-year-old, or any other female ever relied on facts to make their point.

That is one of the reasons why they won most of the arguments.

In the end, I forced a compromise. If I brought Sandy a new outfit, Taylor would allow me to buy her two of the toys in the cart. Not sure where I came out winning in the compromise, but at least to Taylor, the conditions were acceptable.

Taylor picked out an art set and a stuffed animal. Sandy showed me how when unfolded the animal worked as a pillow, that I could've figured out. But after what Taylor had said about already having a stuffed army bear, I had to wonder about her choice.

"Why the tiger?"

"John said you like tigers, because they play baseball." Taylor didn't have to say she doubted John's story. It was written all over her face.

"John's right this time." I could always explain to her later when we were on better terms. "In Michigan our tigers play baseball."

"How do they hold the bats?"

"In their mouths."

Taylor backed away from me with a "you got to be kidding" look on her face.

It gave John a chance to add a pair of large water guns and a Barbie doll to the haul. When Taylor started to complain, John reminded Taylor that some of the toys were for him. It took a while to convince Taylor on the doll since she had originally picked it out herself, but in the end, John prevailed.

Sandy was a little harder to persuade, but in the end, she accepted a couple of blouses and pair of slacks. When she thought I wasn't looking, Sandy fingered them like they were silk spun from gold. It must have felt good to have something new instead of cast off from the charity bins.

I found a warmth long forgotten welling up, but I hid that from my companions. I didn't want them to think I was going soft. Buying things for a newfound granddaughter was one thing; being nice to an adult stranger was something different.

John talked Sandy into wearing the new clothes to lunch, and again I made the mistake of asking out loud where people wanted to go for late lunch early dinner. Before anyone else could open their mouth to offer a suggestion, Taylor got out McDonald's four times. Sandy tried to frown out a no, but I stopped her. I was already on thin ice with the young lady and did not want to push it.

In her new clothes, Sandy was the sharpest-dressed lady in the place even though several business people had stopped by to grab a bite. John's size and acquired sense of army neat made a nice accompaniment to Sandy's look.

And Taylor?

Clothes did not matter with her. When Taylor broke out her smile, everyone within sight fell under her enchantment. Not a bad one from the fairy tales but the type that reached into your heart and filled it the warmth of homemade soup on a cold winter day.

A perfect family, except for the grumpy old fourth wheel following behind.

Since my retirement, I had dressed for my comfort and could have cared less what other people saw. I ran a finger across my chin and realized I could use a shave, and looking down told me the jeans I was wearing could have been newer.

I would have to take care of my appearance in the near future, but first I had other trails to check out. While the young people did a repeat performance in the playroom, I took advantage of the time to get on my laptop.

When I grew up computers took up whole walls, and information was stored on huge reels it took a pair of outstretched arms to handle. What the young kids accept as normal was just one step above magic to me. Junior had become my computer tech at an early age, and he ended up setting down the house rules.

If it had involved adding or subtracting from any of the installed computer programs, don't do it.

"Leave it for him!"

If it had involved a download, don't do it.

"Leave it for him!"

If it had involved anything new, don't try it.

Wait for him to explain it, usually several times and then quite often. It still was a "Don't do it!"

When Junior left for the army, I had to start learning things on my own. Through trial and error, I managed to become so-so on the computer. Usually took me forty-five minutes or so to do what my daughter could complete in less than five.

So it came as no surprise to me when I could not find anything on the computer about the Church of Our Father. I found some that were close, but none exactly right or in this part of the East.

I even tried COOF and COO father. Got nothing but some off-the-wall business that had nothing to do with religion. By then even Taylor had grown tired of the playroom and was ready to leave. I was able to ignore Taylor's first tug, but the second and third got a lot sharper.

Finally, I slapped the laptop shut and gave Taylor my "upset with you" look.

The look worked like a charm.

Taylor broke off tugging my sleeve and laughed at me. She seemed to think my scary face was funny.

So much for grandparental control, but getting a smile again from Taylor was worth it.

Who cared what the Church of Our Father was really about?

I did.

Chapter 28

DIDN'T HAVE TIME TO DO any more lab work after McDonald's but did squeeze in a phone call to my daughter while making a gas stop on the edge of town. I encouraged the ladies to make a rest stop, and with John pumping the fuel, I was free for a few moments.

The daughter answered on the second ring.

"Hi, brat."

"Hi, Daddy. How is the trip going?"

"Different."

"Sounds about right for you."

If nothing else, my girls knew me.

Both of them had been raised by their mother, my first wife, but had remained daddy's girl. Neither of them or Junior permitted the term *half sibling* to be used to descript their relationship. Anyone doing so was corrected politely the first time, with the second correction, when needed, being less than polite. As a trio, my kids were beyond close, and they took care of their old man.

Each in their own way.

"Doing anything important?"

"I'm babysitting with my nieces." I heard the rumble of their play in the background and smiled. "But that is an easy task. I just threaten them with their Paw Paw, and they behave."

"Before or after they get done laughing?"

"After."

After our chuckling broke down, my daughter got serious. And since neither of the girls approved of my search, she broke the subject barrier I figured would be my job.

"Did you find what you were looking for?"

"And more!" I drew back an inch from the mouth piece, as if to distance myself from what I had to say. "Taylor is a girl."

"Sorry, but I suspected as much."

"You could have told me."

"You wouldn't have listened." I heard the tenseness in her voice, but the words which came next were meant to be heartfelt. "But the girls can use another cousin, male or female."

"Thank you, I know how hard it is for you to say that."

"Dad, we can't handle your need for answers." Old argument which would have led to the same ending. "But it doesn't mean we don't love you or miss Junior."

I could have carried that conversation much further, but John was waving from the pump to signal his completion, and the girls would be back any moment. It was time to push forward the real meaning of my call.

"I need you to do me a favor."

"Which is?"

"Some computer research on a local church." I drew in a breath, trying to hide my feelings. I didn't need another round of concern over my behavior, even if she would probably be right. "It is not a big deal, but I drew a blank with my own search."

"Does it have to do with Taylor?"

"In a way." I wanted to explain further but was cut off.

"Give me the name."

"Church of Our Father."

"Do they go by any other names?"

"Not that I know of."

I got a long pause and thought I heard the scratch of writing in the background. I figured my girl was either writing down the name or her latest kitchen creation. I was hoping for the church name.

"I'll get with sis and see what we can do."

"Thanks, babe."

"Love you, Daddy!"

I started to reply with an "I love you too" of my own when a thought hit me.

"The name is written different on their sign."

"Different spelling?"

"No, but there is only a capital *C* written down for church."

"That's strange."

"Probably nothing, but when you asked about a different name." I trailed off feeling stupid for bringing it up.

"Dad, I don't know why, but I think I want to start checking this out right now."

She was brushing me off, and I didn't blame her. This seemed to becoming one hell of a wild-goose chase.

"Tell the little ones I love them."

"Will do. And, Dad."

"Yes."

"You be careful."

"Always. Love you, kid."

"Love you too, Dad, and remember be careful."

Chapter 29

EATING ON OUR RETURN WAS not really needed, and the evening chow down became more snack than meal.

Sandy's streak of motherhood might have yearned for more, but Taylor was barely able to stay awake. At least three times, I noticed Taylor's head faded toward the cheese and crackers on the coffee table, the last time actually falling into it.

Afterward, Taylor claimed a lack of fatigue and fought Sandy's urging to find her bed. I stepped in and told Sandy not to worry, giving her a wink on the side away from Taylor.

Twenty-five minutes later, I was carrying my granddaughter into her room. Sandy followed to help, and I stepped back while she did all the blanket tucking. It was only after Taylor was happily curled into a ball that I leaned over to kiss her forehead.

"Junior told me about the forehead kiss."

"I thought he was too young to remember."

"He heard you mention it to a friend, and he saw you in action with his nieces on your last visit."

"Junior told you quite a bit."

"Junior wanted kids." Sandy looked back at her daughter. "And wanted to raise them, just like his father."

"Father is a wide-raising term, including a lot of men and a lot of different parenting."

I tried to make light of the moment to quell the tightness gathering in my chest and throat. Only Sandy would have none of it. She had to twist the memories in further like a dull drill bit.

"With Junior, there was only person worthy of being called Father."

"But I failed to protect him."

"No, you didn't, but if you feel that way; make it up to him by protecting Taylor, his daughter and your granddaughter."

I had missed John's entrance, but his words were a lot harder to ignore.

Chapter 30

J UST WHAT I NEEDED TO hear: the perfect way to get rid of my survivor guilt. All I had to do was pile on the "you are a jerk" guilt.

As we retreated into the living room, I realized I didn't have the energy or emotions to discuss the past or future much further. Instead, I made up excuses about needing some rest after a long day.

Like a six year could ever wear me out, again?

John made a motion to come with me, but I objected to ruining his evening. He pointed out a need of clean clothes by holding his shirt out away from his body, and sniffing at it. We both knew the rest of his clothes were resting in his room back at the inn, but I wanted to be alone.

I think John was more interested in preventing my brooding alone than clothes, but he had a point I couldn't refute. At least until Sandy brought up the fact that we had a second means of transportation setting in her driveway.

It was an ugly color, but I was not going to be the one driving it.

I had my Ranger.

Going around the first corner, I slowed down to a crawl, checking out the shadows for watchers. I did not see any, but without coming to a complete stop and getting out of the ranger, I could not be sure.

Maybe our Mr. Father had learned to trust us.

More likely Salem's crew had not yet reacted to our return.

At any rate, their absent gave me a good reason to relaxed and enjoy the ride. At least until I got back to my room.

The room looked a lot like it had this morning. You could see where room service had been at work, replacing the towels, making the bed, and tidying up. But it felt wrong.

Stuff moved, which should not have been touched. A dirty shirt from yesterday, which should have been on the chair, had moved to the tabletop. When I picked it up, I found it was right side out.

A possible occurrence, but doubtful, ninety-nine times out of a hundred, my T-shirts came off with a tug over the head and toss toward the dirty clothes. I didn't remember last night being the odd one out of a hundred.

Checking out the rest of my stuff, I found the travel bag disturbed. Instead of being left half zipped, it was closed all the way. I was lucky to remember zipping the bag when I was traveling, let alone while it was sitting in a hotel room.

And last but not least, I check my duffel bag. Clothes nice and neat refolded a lot like the way I folded them, except for the fact I never folded my dirty clothes. They went into the bag in a roughed-up ball or roll.

Sandy answered her phone on the third ring and chatted for a moment or so while John dragged himself away his relax time in front of the tube. At least I hoped so; I did not need any youthful romancing added on to my problems.

"John, I want you to come back to the inn."

"Planned on it."

"I need you to come back now."

John hesitated, either thinking over my question or checking to see if Sandy was in hearing range. "Why?"

"Either our present abode has the best maid service in the state or some moron searched my room." I gave it a second to sink in and finished, "I was wondering if your room got the same service."

"Somebody is going to be sorry, if they did."

I left my door open, hoping to catch the sounds of John approaching. I shouldn't have bothered. With his angry stomp, I would have heard John coming down the hall with earplugs and a pillow over my head.

John might have been doing a double time but sounded more like a bayonet charge going downhill. By the time I got to the doorway, John was already sticking the room key into the lock. It turned over with a click from the last century, but John went in with the modern anger of today.

It took John all of six seconds to come to the same conclusion as me. Nothing was missing or really disturbed, but at the same time, the rooms felt as if victimized by a minor earthquake.

I waited semi-patient until John's fury dropped to a more reasonable level. It took a good sixty-five seconds and an emotional five gallons of imaginary steam.

"Got any guesses who?"

"Father?"

"More likely than Taylor or Sandy."

"You can be such a smart-ass." John actually smiled. "Just like your son."

I should have corrected John's comment. Correctly speaking, Junior was just like me since he was born second. But it didn't seem important at that moment.

"Doubt if Father would have taken the chance of being caught."

"Salem?"

"We wouldn't have caught on."

"You think Salem is one slick lady." John rubbed at the daily growth on his jaw and came to my guess. "You're probably right, so it has to be one of the goons watching us?"

John didn't need a nod of confirmation, so I went on to the next point.

"And those guys are sloppy enough to be noticed." I picked at an old water stain on the room's bureau. "We might want to check that out tomorrow."

"And then?"

"If it was one of them." I cracked a nail against the water stain. "I think we deserve some answers."

John grinned, thinking the same thing as me.

Chapter 31

WE BOTH WOULD HAVE RATHER done our checking at once, but I realized the cleaning crew would be the best people to ask. They would not be in until tomorrow, and I did not want to leave Sandy and Taylor alone until then.

It took a while, but I finally convinced John to put off checking out until the next day. He did gather up most of his stuff before leaving and even offered to take my dirty clothes with him for a Laundromat run.

I begged off, having brought more clothes than John. That was one of the things I liked about bringing my truck, I could carry more without paying for it. But more important than clean clothes, I wanted John back at Sandy's, protecting my granddaughter.

Yeah, I knew Taylor would be all right. Sandy was a good mother and would not let anything happen to her, voluntarily, but what if they came in a group?

And what if Father was one of those religious nuts who brainwashed young kids?

Or Salem might be a girl who could not have babies? Maybe she was just biding her time, waiting for a chance to make a grab and run.

And then again, maybe I had watched too many news programs.

Seemed like the media dug up a new and improved nut case each and every week to scare the public. Most of the nut cases I knew were harmless like me, because there was no doubt in my mind that I was one. To take on being a single father and actually loving the job, I had to be a nut case.

Right about mid thought, I got a knock at my door.

I almost ignored the knock but figured John must have a good reason to come back so soon. I knew there was no way John could have gotten to Sandy's and back, no matter how fast he drove. He must have forgotten something and needed the room key he had left with me.

Still I took my time getting over to the door and expected a second knock to hurry me along. John had not left in a patience mood, but the expected second knock never came. And when I threw open the door?

It wasn't John.

Chapter 32

S ALEM WALKED OVER TO MY bed without even a "Do you mind if I come in?" and slipped into a comfortable, stretched-out position. It was kind of like sitting, but not really. The position was more of a curled up lean on to one hip.

"Would you like to come in?" My tone and smart-assed expression should have brought up a response.

Instead Salem ignored my comment, rubbing her left hand over a slightly parted pair of lips. I almost felt like it was her room and I was the guest, but I wasn't given a profession smart-ass cup by the local bank for nothing.

"Oh, sorry, you are already in."

Salem rubbed her hand over the lips a second time and gave me the most superior look I had ever gotten from a human. Salem's look made me feel like I had forgotten to feed the cat.

"Did Taylor enjoy McDonald's?"

"If not, she did a real good job of faking it."

"I'm glad." Salem slipped both legs up on to the bed, causing her to lean even further to one side. "Taylor deserves more good times than she gets."

"Taylor seems happy enough to me."

"Because she is a special little lady, which is why she deserves more."

Couldn't argue with the lady and didn't want to prolong the conversation anyway.

"It took you a long time for breakfast."

"Not really, but we shopped and stayed for a late lunch."

I wanted to declare it was none of Salem's business how long we took for breakfast but found myself trying to stay polite. I did not need to crank up the old blood pressure any further. I'm sure it was already up into the danger zone because of my room search.

"Father was worried that you might have left for good."

"Because we had his car?"

"Because you had Taylor." Salem's demeanor tensed, not badly, but I was watching close enough to notice. "Father has other cars, but Taylor is unique."

"Taylor is a little girl, and Father does not own her."

"Some people think they own everything."

"Some people are wrong."

"Wrong people can be dangerous." Salem took a moment to study the back of her hand again as if it were the most important thing in her world. "Especially those who think they have power."

"Are you bringing me a threat from your Father?"

"He doesn't know I'm here."

"Are you threatening me?"

Salem gave me a look dropping my IQ by at least fifty points.

"If I was going to make a threat, I would have targeted Sandy." Salem glanced out the crack between the windows curtains. "Or if desperate, John."

"But not me?"

Salem's dropped my IQ another ten points before answering.

"You are not the type to take a threat well."

"You think I might call your bluff?"

"I know you would." I started to grin in spite of myself, but Salem added the killer. "You are just like Junior."

"You knew my son?"

"Only through Sandy, but that is enough to tell me you both came from the same mold."

"Is that good or bad?"

"It is what it is." Salem stuck out just the tip of her tongue. "But it does means I am not bringing you a threat."

"What are you bringing me?"

"A piece of knowledge." Salem hopped off my bed and made for the door. "Use it to aid Taylor."

Chapter 33

WELL, I DIDN'T WANT TO sleep much anyway.

It was much more fun to toss and turn the whole night while trying to figure out whether Salem had warned me, set me up, or was just checking me out as a possible sex partner. After all, Salem did seem to like older men. I had to be at least ten years younger than Father and hopefully better-looking. Of course, after another night of rest-free sleep, that age gap might have strung to five or even less.

I finally gave up and hit the shower to start out my day and then hit John's room. It didn't look as if it had been touched a second time.

Then after removing the last of John's gear to my room, I checked him out of his room and questioned a clerk sporting the name tag Fred about Father and his people. The conversation quickly moved me from the status of half-welcomed stranger to intrusive outsider within the first few utterances.

"Ever heard of the Father?"

Fred the clerk's faked smiled disappeared like a glass of Scotch at an AA meeting.

"We have a resident of our city called that."

"Do you know him by sight?"

"Everyone does."

I had to hold off a moment while Fred answered the desk phone. After clicking off, he took his time getting back to me, making it oblivious he did not want to rejoin our talk.

"Has he been around?"

"Father does not stay at our inn." Again, Fred the clerk made to dismiss me, this time by burying his head in his paperwork.

"Should I take my questions to your manager?" I reached down to grab Fred's hand.

"He wouldn't have time for you."

"Probably." I flipped over my wrist to make sure Fred saw my remembrance band. "But then again your manager might be interested in your behavior toward customers, especially those with military connections."

I could see the wanted words playing beneath the professionalism of his job, and the paycheck overriding them. "The Father does not care for our menu and, to the best of my knowledge, has never been in any other part of the inn."

"And his people?"

"Are not encouraged to visit." Fred glanced around, checking for eavesdroppers. "But this is a public place, and Father's people are around here all too often, especially the silver-haired young lady."

"Did you see any of them around yesterday?"

"None of the men, but Miss Salem walked through in the morning." Fred the clerk glanced down a final time at my wristband and then shrugged to himself. "She is the only one who does not give me the creeps."

We chatted a little more, but Fred did not have much more to add.

It was nine o'clock, and I figured ten or so before the cleaning crew started working the rooms. In the meantime, I settled down in the cafe and waited for John to show up.

The service was worse yet.

I was ignored for better than ten minutes, and my order was so messed up I almost skipped eating it. My over-medium eggs came back with enough white gung floating on the plate to wonder if the eggs had touched the grill for more than a touchdown and flip over. The sausage links were pretty well-blacken with well-split skin and dried-out innards, yet they managed to be accompanied by a crap load of fresh grease.

I had eaten worse, but not on purpose.

Getting back to my room, I found the cleaning crew going in and out of a room midway down the hall with towels and sheets. John was doing a team knock at my door.

It was the team knock kept me from waving John down to me. I found myself wanting to hold Taylor more than go through another hostile question and answer conversation, especially with Taylor listening.

Chapter 34

WITH JOHN'S HELP AFTER HE spotted me coming down the hall and approaching on tiptoes, I was able to get within poking distance of Taylor. As the knocking teams reached forward to repeat the knock, I put a fingertip in each side of Taylor just below the rib cage. Taylor's jump almost took her out of John's arms, and then she turned to me with a giggling frown.

"Granpa!"

"Yes?"

"That's no way to answer a door."

"I am not answering the door." I held out my hands, and Taylor lurched toward me. "I'm sneaking up on my granddaughter."

"Don't do it again!"

"Why not?"

"Because . . ." Taylor's sly grin came peeking out. "I like being teased by you, and telling you to stop will keep you doing it."

I gave Taylor my best bear hug and whispered past her ear to John.

"The boys who date Taylor are going to be in trouble."

"You think!" John's smile stretched out another level into a laugh as Taylor snapped her head around to see what he was saying. "She already has a couple of old guys wrapped around her little fingers."

"Anyone I know?"

"Well, she talked one of them into bringing her here to help gather up my gear."

"Glad I am not the other." I let Taylor slide down my leg as I used the key to open the door. "I moved your stuff in here and checked you out."

Giving John the last bit of information gave Taylor time to dart into the room ahead of us. John and I gave each other a look, laughed, and followed Taylor into the room, but I don't think either of us expected to see our energy ball standing dead still.

"Taylor?"

"I smell Salem."

"She's here?" John stepped forward to put his body between Taylor and the room.

"No, silly." Taylor threw her hands up on to both hips. "I smell Salem. I don't see her."

"You mean Salem's perfume," John relaxed as he turned back to Taylor and went down on one knee. "A lot of women wear the same perfume."

"No, not perfume. Salem has her own smell."

"John!"

John's head came around with the patronizing grin he had been using on Taylor. I wiped that look away with my next words.

"Salem was here last night."

"I told you so." Taylor added a foot stomp to her stance as an accent to the point.

"She stopped by to give me some advice."

"Was Salem here for the whole night?" John's comment was leading toward sexual with an attitude hard to read. It might have been a mixture of protective and disturbed, with a touch of envy.

"Ten minutes tops with no touching."

"You should have brushed her hair, Granpa, Salem likes it, especially if you use your fingers."

Taylor's last addiction to the conversation ratcheted up my tension to low-level heart pounding. Salem was not a bad-looking lady, and I was human. I didn't think I was attracted to her, but Salem was mysterious, and like most men, I loved a mystery.

Maybe I was seeing shadows just to be around here, or . . .

I didn't finish the *or* thought because of an interruption at the door.

Chapter 35

THE CLEANING LADY STICKING HER head in was barely past high school. She hadn't yet learned to keep her smile in check around guests, and when Taylor bounced over to say hi, it came out full force.

"Hello, little lady!"

"Are you here to visit my granpa?"

"No." The young girl went down on knee to be closer to the questioner. "I am here to clean his room."

"Couldn't he clean his own?" Taylor wiggled her nose back and forth. "I have to clean mine."

"Your grandfather is older." She leaned forward to stage whisper into Taylor's ear. "He needs the help."

"Okay."

Taylor took the maid's hand and walked her further into the room.

"I can come back later, sir."

"No need," John leaned forward to read the name tag or get a better view I am not sure which. "Nadeen. We were about to leave."

"I'll help my mother across the hall and then come back when you leave."

The word mother dampened down John's lean, but not his conversation.

"By the way, were you working yesterday?"

"Yes." The warmth washed out of Nadeen's smile. "But I do not steal."

"Didn't think you had." John turned on the charm with limited effects. "Your smile is too honest to steal."

"Then why do you ask?"

"Just wonder about the people hanging around our rooms."

"You mean strangers." Nadeen's smile was completely gone.

"Or townspeople that had no reason to be here."

"My daughter should not be talking to you."

Ma looked a lot like an older edition of Nadeen with visibility more wear and pounds. Also the elder's face held no smile or warmth. I knew it would take more than masculine charm to get an answer out of this lady. Time to take over for John, but not in the way he would have expected.

I moved forward to gather up my strangely quiet granddaughter, ignoring the daughter and turning to the mother instead. I rocked back and forth a couple of times and let Taylor wrap both arms around my neck with her head on my shoulder.

"Sorry." I bounced a little flat-footed to focus Ma's captured attention on Taylor. "We were wrong to bother your daughter, but John is very protective of Taylor."

"She is a cutie."

"And I do not want any perverts hanging around."

"Nadeen, do the other room."

So much for my questioning tactic, but Ma didn't leave. She studied Taylor with the intensity of a mother bear and the same temperament. It seemed like twenty minutes before she spoke again, but I knew better. Nadeen had barely cleared the room before the mother opened her mouth.

"Fred told me of your questions." The glance back over the shoulder at a disappearing daughter told me of her instincts. "And I should not get involved."

"But?"

"I noticed the Father's pet was down the hall at the intersection." The words came out as spit and continued heavy dose of fury. "I kept a watch on her as I worked."

"And did Salem approach my room."

I tilted my head to the side straining to hear the words more clearly if possible.

"She never came any closer than the corner."

Unless she came back later in the day or had already searched ours rooms before picking up the father. That might have explained the sloppiness, but I did not think so. From what the maid was saying, it was more likely Salem was standing watch.

"And Salem's merry crew of church members."

"I never saw any of them." Ma's voice dripped of hot pepper juice. "But that doesn't mean they were not around."

The words might not have burned a hole in the floor, but if dropped, I am betting on a heavy scarring. Personally, I would not have wanted to have them aimed in my direction and had to wonder what brought out such venom.

Being a guy, I had to ask.

"Do you have something against the Father and his people?"

She gave a look at Taylor to remind me about little pictures with big ears, and I could have kicked myself for forgetting my granddaughter's presence. Of course in my defense, it had been a long time since I had to worry about little eavesdroppers.

"Can I pick out my towels?"

"They have different colors?"

Taylor's head popped up like a jack-in-the-box, proving she had been listening.

"Just difference softness?"

"Can I help pick them out?"

"I have a better idea." I focused totally on my granddaughter's eyes, were checking to see if I was trying to put one past her. "Why don't you and John pick out the towels while I help this nice lady make my bed?"

Chapter 36

TAYLOR LEFT THE ROOM, LEANING back, not really trying to hear because kids at her age do not really eavesdrop. Right, and they never put on a sad face or happy smile to influence our actions.

My companion stepped over to my bed and began straightening out the remembrance of my restless sleep.

"I should not be talking to a stranger."

"And I should not have to worry about my granddaughter's safety."

With a practiced hand sweep, she straightened out the last wrinkles of my sheets and tugged at the blanket. Getting it in shape would require several adjustments.

"Father is not liked around here."

"Because of his religion?"

"Because he is creepy, and I am not sure his church is a religion."

"Why would you say that?"

"Father doesn't allowed locals to join. He preaches out of a lodge, and his followers have no personality."

From what I saw, that sounded about right.

"Does everyone in town feel the same?"

"I don't know everyone." Nadeen's mother leaned into the bed to fluff the pillows. "But among the people I know, their opinions are usually harsher than mine."

"So asking about them?"

"Is not making you any friends," With a swish the pillows were covered and I had a bed ready for tonight's visit.

"Why don't you run him out of town?"

I was kidding. The maid's answer was not.

"It has been discussed, but . . ."

"He's rich."

Her brown eyes drilled right into my skull and left me wishing I had never started this conversation. I started to reach out a hand to hold back her next utterance but was too late.

"Father seems to have a moneyed interest in everything, either inherited or bought into when the economy took a dip." Her eyes gleamed with deadness beyond emotion. "But I could handle that."

Then how does a little old man upset a whole town. I didn't want it to be fear, especially my fear. The one eating at the back of my mind like a tumor I couldn't cure.

"My friends could handle Father owning the town." A tear seemed to be forming in the corner of her eye. "The whole town could handle him owning us. We have seen worse."

I needed to reach out and stop her, but I couldn't. It was like leaning out over a cliff. I knew better, but I wanted to see the bottom.

"We're scared of him."

"He is a little old man!"

"He looks at our little girls, and it isn't right."

"Sexual?"

"No, it is worse." The tears were edging out and in danger of falling. "It is a cold, frozen look, like the snake watching the mouse."

The next word I heard was the worse, but it came from neither of us. "Granpa?"

Chapter 37

I T TOOK LUNCH, A TRIP to the local shoe store for a pair of shoes matching grandpa's, bracketed by two trips to the playground to take Taylor's mind off the Father. When we finally got her home, it was pushing five, and Sandy had just returned from cleaning houses. I had offered to make up the difference of taking a day off, but Sandy's pride would not allow it.

Taylor greeted her mother with a half-felt hug and plunked herself on the couch with a childish sigh. A minute later, Taylor was on her side and sleeping. John was into the yellow pages part of the process for ordering take-out, and Sandy was about to take off for the shower.

Me?

I was about to upset all their plans with the announcement of my plans for the evening. Plans I was sure Sandy and John would be unhappy with and plans I was even more sure had to be followed

"I need the address of Father's church."

"Why?" Sandy stopped turning the knob to the bathroom door with the handle half twisted.

"I want to check out his church."

"Father won't like that." It was John speaking, but Sandy's frightened nod was in agreement. "I doubt if he will let you in."

"I'm not going to ask him."

"If you get caught, Father might take it out on Taylor and me."

"Then I won't get caught." Sandy's expression told me of her doubts, so I added the coming truth. "Besides, you and Taylor are going to be out of this town beyond the reach of Father within the month."

"You're taking Taylor."

"I'm going to help you get out of here."

Not really the answer Sandy wanted to hear, but the best I was willing to offer. John was another matter.

"I'm going with you."

"I want you here with Sandy and Taylor."

"Doesn't matter." John pulled out his wallet and handed Sandy a couple of bills. "We will be back before dark, so order some pizzas when Taylor wakes up."

"John!" I stepped forward to stress my point. "You're military. You get caught, and the army might get upset."

"As you said, then we won't get caught."

Chapter 38

FATHER'S PLACE OF WORSHIP LOOKED to be more doctor's office than church. There were no steeples or stained-glass windows. And as far as I could see, there was no cross or religious symbol of any kind on the building.

It swung long and low for the length of half a city block. The bricks were of a mud color with few windows and no beauty. The door I would have expected to be on the street end of the building was at the midblock end without a parking lot to invite people in.

I saw Father's beat-up pickup was parked on the street with two other cars, neither of which looked to be anything special. Apparently, Father picked his cars and buildings more for use than flash. Another time and place, I might have liked the idea. Nowadays, too many of the people spreading God's Word were more flash than message.

I checked out the windows from across the street.

There were four windows on the end closest to the street. They were small and up high on the wall. I am not sure even John on tiptoes would be high enough to peek in. Getting hoisted up high enough to get in those were also out of the question.

I was too wide to go through the window. Even though John was a bit slimmer, there was no way I could have lifted him high enough to reach the window without breaking my back in a dozen places.

There was one more window halfway up the length of the building. It was larger, and with aid from John, I could have wiggled through. Or I could let John use his army training to get in and open the door for me. Either way, it might attract attention from any one driving past, but as a last resort, we could come back after dark and try it.

"Do you want to try checking out the windows on the other side?"

"Why not try the door?"

"In this neighborhood, it will be locked."

"Might not be." John tapped my shoulder to get my full attention. "And if we get caught, we can always claim we were just checking to see if we could use the car for another out-of-town run."

"And you expect Father and his crew to believe it?"

"Don't care." John leaked out a meaner-than-evil smile, and I begin to think John would not mind getting caught. "What is Father going to do, call me a liar?"

I took a look at John's fat-free body.

I was not about to call John a liar, and Father was smaller and older than me. If Father had half a brain, he might think John was lying, but he wouldn't say a thing.

And I had yet to see anyone in Father's crew who would match up with John. And I had been fairly handy in my younger days, at the very least I could keep one or two of Father's people busy while John finished off the rest.

"The door is going to be locked."

"Does it hurt to check?"

"We might miss the pizza." I tilted my head to the side and tried to match John's evil grin. "Let's go down a couple blocks and cross over."

It was still light outside, but with no one is sight, we didn't need to sneak up to Father's building. And besides we would look awful silly if someone saw us acting strange or worse turned us into the cops.

John and I made like strollers going down the sidewalk and chatting like we were talking about baseball. When we reached Father's place we went up the sidewalk as if we belonged.

The door was one with a slide bar on the inside like those used in schools. It didn't take much to keep them locked, so the odds just went up against us doing it the easy way. As John hesitated by the door to check the street again, I took a few more steps to see the other side Father's church. I was almost halfway to the corner when John whispered me back.

"Hey, Pops." I looked over my shoulder to find him holding an open door with a grin telling me, "I told you so!"

I should have listened to both him and Sandy.

Going through the door, I found very little, and yet a lot I did not expect.

Chapter 39

THE FIRST ROOM STRETCHED OUT in front of me for over half the length of the building. It contained no pews or chairs, so I guess Father preached to a standing room only crowd. With Father's apparent lack of followers, I would have thought they would be plenty of room for sitting. Unless of course Father had a hidden army of empty-headed goons that no one had ever seen. And I personally did not see that as a realistic possibility.

At least I hoped it wasn't.

Something else bothered me about the room.

There were only two windows in this room, both at the far end and about two thirds of the way up the wall facing each other. They did not let in a whole lot of light, but I had seen halls with less.

I didn't think it was the windows setting off the tingling in the back of my skull.

It couldn't be the walls; they were all empty. There wasn't a cross or religious symbol of any kind in the room. There was not even a shadow imprint where a picture might have hung. It was if the room was unused for anything but cover.

And when I thought about it, there was the problem.

What church keeps a building just for looks?

Perhaps Father's church.

"Want to look in the back?"

"Sure, but I think I know what we are going to find."

"A bunch of gay guys who hate women?" John's smile came up on cue with the words, but it looked a bit forced.

There were four rooms in the back third of the building, and I was wrong. I figured they would be empty, but one was used for storage with the next one being a bathroom cleaned and stocked. It was the two rooms on the other side of the hallway that were more interesting.

The room closest to the main room was the church's office.

But you had to be generous with your wording to label it as an office.

Again, there were no symbols or painting of any kind. The lone object of decoration was a six-foot-long planter filled with frag-ile-looking vines sporting delicate little flowers, white with red trim around each of the petals. They spewed out of the planter in every direction, with vine going up and out the open window.

For a second, I itched at a though and wondered.

What if the plants were coming in the window instead of out?

Would it make a difference?

Was this visit pushing me over the edge?

I didn't think so, but I had to wonder.

Shaking off the thought, I went back to looking over the room. There was a desk pushed up against one wall, with a file cabinet to either side. One was full height containing four drawers; the other had two drawers only with the top coming level with the desktop. It was the two drawer one I would have liked to check out, but it had a security system beyond normal.

It had a double-bar-style lock holding both drawers in place, with a heavy-metal-style strapping going around the sides. I could have smashed the lock holding the bars in place or burned the bands off with a torch. But with this being a walk-in break-in, I did not have the needed equipment. I wasn't sure where I would find such equipment, and if I did?

Dragging heavy equipment into Father's church would have attracted way too much attention.

I rifled through the file in the big cabinet, but it was all forms. Most of them were headed COO Father, or C of Our Father, but none of them were labeled with the word *church*. It was like Father hated the word, but what else could *C* stand for? *Cult*, that was a dirty word, and no one in their right mind would consider calling their group a cult.

Of course, no one so far had claimed Father was sane.

The desk was a dead zone.

Even the desk pad was free of doodles, and the top drawer was empty except for pens, stamps, and blank envelopes. It had plenty of room for more junk, but there just wasn't any stuff, not even a paperclip. The bottom drawers? They were more of the same only more so, a dust mite would have gotten lonely.

The last room was being used as a bedroom.

At first, I suspected Father, but the clothes were female. Using the hold-them-up method, I guess they were Salem's. There was nothing fancy about them, but all were nice and well cared for.

Even without a chest of drawers or closet in sight.

They were all neatly hung or folded with the folded clothes stacked in several milk cartons. The six cartons being used were formed into a pyramid against the outside wall, with the hanging clothes to the right. There they were hung from an old-fashioned wardrobe mover like the ones we had used in high school drama. Nothing more than a few bars on rollers.

Even the bed was simple.

A queen-sized mattress set on the floor, with another milk carton for a bed stand. It looked more like the set up for a pet than a trusted employee. I wonder if Father's own living arrangements would have proved so sparse. I was betting even his goons were treated better.

Of course, for all I knew, these living arrangements were temporary or all the church could afford. As we backed away from the room, John's shaking head told me he doubted such an answer.

"Creepy?"

"Different." But I had to admit John's description was closer to the truth. "Want to leave?"

"Definitely."

They might have been more to see, but I had no idea where to look or what to look for. We had come here to answer questions, and I am sure we did. Just not sure which ones and whether they were the ones we were asking.

Didn't help we had another question waiting with our exit.

"Pops!" John stopped me before I could push out the door. "I locked these behind us."

"Are you sure?"

"Very." John leaned out a hand to push at the door frame, and it swung open. "I wanted to make sure we would hear anyone coming in after us."

"Are you positive?"

I didn't want to doubt John or ask a second time, but I was hoping he was wrong.

"I checked by pushing twice on all four doors."

The look we exchange said it all, and both of us were happy to be clearing out of Father's church and heading back to Sandy's.

Chapter 40

DUSK WAS ROLLING IN AS we reached our destination, but even in the poor light of a shadowed porch, I could see Sandy had a visitor. I should have been surprised, but barely managed a whispered "Oh" in my mind.

"How is my favorite grandfather?"

Salem came down the steps like the queen of jungle cats and brushed against me as she walked past me to gather in John's arm. With an "I just ate your pet bird" look, she back-pivoted to move into the slot between us and gathered in my arm as well.

"Better watch it." In spite of myself, I smiled back at Salem. "You might make your real grandfather jealous."

"Never met him." Salem's grin stretched wider to include a second bird or mouse. "The males of my family don't stay around to help with the kids."

"Hard on the females."

"The women of my bloodline have always been tough." Salem switched her attention back to John, who was beginning to disengage his arm. "Does that scare you?"

I knew what John's answering look would be, even before it flashed on to his face. Instead of watching it, I glanced over at Sandy standing at the bottom of the porch.

She seemed to have shed a few years since our arrival and tonight's greeting brought out a lot more smile lines and less of the ingrained frown. I found their duel greeting lifting my mood until I noticed the flowers.

They were growing around the front of the house and were white with a crimson trim.

No big deal. The same flowers were often popular in certain areas of the country, but I liked flowers and took a notice of them. Yet I could not remember seeing this type before, and now I found myself noticing them twice in one day. It didn't seem quite right.

"Cute flowers." I used my free arm to wave toward the white blooms, which seemed to be getting brighter and multiplying. "I have never seen anything quite like them before."

"Sure you have."

"They're local and only come out at night."

Sandy's comment jumped over Salem's but could not overpower the "I know something" look on Salem's face. I think I knew the something too, but not sure if I wanted to admit it.

"Most plants bloom in the day."

"Most plants are not living around here."

"Most everything normal is not living here."

Salem smiled at John and tugged us toward the porch.

"We have the pizza ordered." Sandy stepped forward to take my offered hand. "And your granddaughter is in the tub in case we have another attack of too much grandpa time."

"It was John's fault." My sudden movement got me loose of Salem's grip, and I jabbed a finger at the big guy. "He's the toy of the group."

"Only because you're an old fart."

"Hey, took me a long time to become an old fart." I reached out to take Sandy's hand and found myself catching a wet bundle of energy instead.

"Hey, kid, you could have dried off first." I uttered the words through Taylor's hair as I hugged her close. "I'm not going any place for a while."

"I got my clothes on and rubbed off with a towel."

Not sure if Taylor missed the order of or was explaining why she was so wet. Either way, I was just happy to hold her and was not going to put her down, wet or dry.

"Pizza is here."

"Let's go pay for it." I bounced Taylor toward my other side so I could grab my wallet, but I never got a chance as Salem came back into my sight line.

"Already taken care." Salem released John's arm and reached out for Taylor. "Call it a gift from Father, which I will tell him about next time I see him."

John was in a trot toward the pizza delivery car, with Sandy trailing along to his rear. So neither saw Taylor's cling to my neck or Salem's smile fade, not all the way but enough to show her disappointment.

"I'm the new toy in town."

"And I'm the old pet."

Salem tried to push the beam level back up, but the smile refused to capture its full essence. I couldn't be sure with Salem's odd-shaped eyes, but there looked to be sadness or old yearning somewhere in their depths.

"Hurts when they drift away, but they always come back." Didn't seem right to be comforting Salem but seemed even more wrong not to try. "Changed a bit, but that's the fun of watching kids grow up."

"They don't always come back."

Salem's words ended the comforting as I remember my own child drifting away to become a man.

Junior hadn't come back.

He just left behind a great big hole in my soul, and maybe I was having trouble hiding it from Salem. And she had no right to see it; no one did.

"By the way, kid, what do they call these flowers?"

I knelt down on one knee to point out the strange blossoms to Taylor. Salem took advantage of my change of height to lean over and listen for Taylor's answer.

"I don't know, but I like them."

"Me too." I fingered the nearest blossom. I found it harder than I had expected. It could have almost been made of plastic or a stiff silk flower. "Be nice to grow some back home."

"They don't move very well."

"A lot of things don't."

"A lot of people don't."

Not sure where the conversation was going, but Salem called it to a halt by adding the flower's name to the mix and walking inside.

"They're called a witch's rose."

Chapter 41

THE PIZZA WAS OKAY, AND as far as I could see, no one had spat into it on the way here. Not saying one of the cooks had not added some extra self-produced fluid before insertion into the oven, but the high temperature of the baking heat should have taken care of it. If not, I had eaten worse when in college.

I took another look at the pizza crust.

At least I hoped I had.

Salem tried to play with Taylor, but Taylor seemed played out. She munched at the crust and curled up next to her grandpa. It took me a while, but by the time we reached the end of the second sitcom on television, I began to catch on. She was more than tired; Taylor was in a mood and not a happy one.

"Smile, kid, or I'll tickle your brains out."

Taylor did not even attempt to smile. Instead, she brought her knees up on to the couch and curled up against me even tighter. I found Taylor's cheek pressed up against my chest as if she were listening for my heartbeat.

"Granpa, are you leaving?"

"I go to the hotel every night."

"Not the hotel." Taylor's nose dug into my chest. "I mean are you leaving?"

"Oh."

I didn't have an answer. I could have stuck with a standardize answer of "Not for a while" or "Yes, but I will be coming back." Either of the two seemed to be a fair answer to Taylor's question. My granddaughter might be only six but had been crapped on enough for twice that many years.

I was not going to add to the pile.

"Yes, I have to go home some time."

"To Michigan?"

"Yes, that is where my house is." I cradled my hand around Taylor's head to comfort her. "I can't live in a hotel all my life."

"You could stay here."

"What about my pets?"

Taylor's twisted her head enough to glance at Sandy sitting beyond us in the rocker. The conversation halted as Taylor studied her mother's face, and it was then I realized everyone in the room was staring at us.

"Mommy?"

"Sorry, babe." I could see Sandy was about to cry. "There is no room."

"Granpa, I don't want you to leave!"

I hugged Taylor in close and rocked us back and forth on the couch. I know men don't cry, but I could not hold them back. The moisture welled up from deep down beyond the moment and leaked out the corner of my eyes.

"Pops!"

"No." I snapped at John a lot harder than I meant to, but it was a snap all the same. "I won't decide Taylor's future on a moment like this."

"Granpa will come back." Sandy barely had two inches of butt remaining on the rocker, and I figured the next rock would dump her into a kneeling position at my feet. "We will see him soon, I promise."

"You can't promise, people leave and don't come back."

Taylor's beg for understanding went to Salem and met the slightest of nod, probably independent of what she wanted to project.

"No."

I cut off Salem's intrusion before the first word could be uttered.

"I won't lie to Taylor." Again, I came out sharper than intended. "She knows people don't always come back."

Everyone got quiet, but even Salem knew I was thinking about Junior. His name clouded over the room without needing to be said.

He left us and had not come back to me, Sandy, John, and most importantly, Taylor.

"I can only promise to be the best granpa possible."

There was nothing left for us to say.

My companions were all fenced in by their own losses and unable to give comfort to me or Taylor. I could only hope Taylor could feel a matching reassuring pressure on her shoulder as the one I could faintly feel on my left shoulder.

It might not have been Junior's physical present, but somewhere inside, I knew he was with me.

Chapter 42

I WOKE UP THE NEXT MORNING still on the couch with most of my gathered cast around me.

Sandy was dozing in the rocker, head tilted to one side with her mouth opened as if getting ready to drool. She didn't look very comfortable, but I guess sleeping in a beat-up old wooden rocker was not the best way to spend a night. John was nowhere in sight, but Salem was curled up at my feet, and I do mean curled up.

Salem had managed to curl herself into a ball with both hands locked together over her legs and her head lying against the outer side of the knee. It was almost as if she was using the knee for a pillow. I didn't see how the position was humanely possible, but I had to be wrong.

Here it was right in front of me. Or was until I looked a second time and found Salem uncurling into a stretch all too sexual for my liking. Well, my liking, considering where I was at, and the age gap. Salem turned the stretch into a pivot, which left her kneeling with both arms folded over my knees.

"Did you sleep sound?"

"Not sure, I haven't tried to stand up yet."

"Kind of hard to do anything with our little salvation clinging to you." Salem nodded toward Taylor still pressed against my chest. "Do you want me to take her so you can get up?"

"No!"

I found myself loving the feel of Taylor against my chest, and after last night's conversation, I did not want to break such a contact. Of course, after Taylor's wiggle around to get more comfortable, my body reminded me there were reasons for breaking contact from another person that had nothing to do with leaving. I changed my no into a yes, with an expression of discomfort and a nod.

Salem rose the rest of the way using a slink of complete control and grace. I wanted to ask how she managed the move, but as Taylor was lifted from my lap, I realized this was not the time for questions and answer. By the time I got back to the living room, Sandy and Taylor were also awake and moving around.

"What happened to John?"

"He went back to the hotel," Salem answered for both women, "Muttering something about wanting to spend the night in a real bed."

"Muttering?" Sandy joined in with a chuckle. "More like full forced bitching."

"John?"

"John!"

The answer came back at me in chorus, and the girls looked at each other. Sandy's chuckle broke into a gale of laugh, and in spite of Salem's best attempt at self-control, she joined in.

I should have told them; I was not surprised by the bitching. It was John leaving that had brought out my comment. After our search of the church, I didn't figure John would let Taylor or Sandy out of his sight for anything. But John did know I was there for the night, and the lure of a good bed had to be awful strong. After just one night in a sitting position, I looked at the couch as a step above Venus flytrap.

I stretched out a cramp in my lower back and added under my breath, "One very tiny step at that."

"Want me to call him back?"

Salem spun out a cell phone one-handed and had her finger over the first number before I had a chance to answer. I started my answer and then held back. A good thing because before I could recommence another voice had to put her two cents' worth in.

"I'm hungry."

Sandy frowned at her daughter, more in pain than displeasure. Feeding four from her pantry had probably been more of a challenge than Sandy wanted the public to know, and having John as a break-fast guest the last couple of days hadn't helped.

"Better idea." I broke out a grin for Taylor which was also meant even more for Sandy. "Call and tell John we will meet him for breakfast."

"At the inn?"

My stomach did a roller-coaster drop and then settled at the bottom like a piece of dried-up Play-Doh. I wasn't sure how bad their food could get, but I didn't really want to find out.

"Any other places in town worth mentioning?"

"For the food or the service?" Sandy gave Salem the eye and passed a secret message. I got the feeling from the look and Salem's tone of voice, she did not get very good service no matter where she ate.

"The food, I'm not a big fan of the service around here."

"Mel's!"

Sandy and Salem went off in unison with Taylor's added her yip a microsecond behind.

"It's a dump, but the food is great."

"And homemade."

"And they treat me to free cookies."

Well, with a review started by Sandy, added to by Salem, and finished by Taylor, I could hardly doubt the truth of it.

"Will John be able to find it?"

"Nope, not a chance." Sandy added a nodded agreement, but Salem went on before I could suggest a contact with John. "But that is no problem. I'll slip by the inn and pick him and your Ranger up."

"You want to drive my Ranger?"

"No."

Salem gave me the evil eye. I guessed she did not like my tone. But I had not forgotten Father's comment about Salem's driving abil-ity and didn't want to test the truth of such a statement. The Ranger was my baby, a reminder of the Ranger I had driven forever before this one.

Junior had learned to drive in my first Ranger, laughing at his friends who had a problem with stick shifts and borrowing it for several moves in and out of my house. During our last conversation, he had asked me again if I was ready to turn it over to him at the end of his deployment.

"John took your Ranger last night so we could have the Father's loaner for the car seat."

"Oh." I didn't mind John driving it, at least not as much as Salem. "Then I'll pick John up while you girls get Taylor ready."

"No way."

Salem was slipping out the door before I could argue. And it was only when she was gone I realized Salem did not have a car. Before I could ask Sandy about it, I had a six-year-old grabbing my hand for some needed wardrobe help.

And at that moment, Taylor seemed more important.

Goes to tell you how easy a guy can be swayed by a pretty face, especially if she is your granddaughter.

Chapter 43

MEL'S WASN'T A DUMP.

But calling it fancy would have been a downright lie.

I could have eaten off the floor, but the flower design of the linoleum faded as you moved away from the wall. In the main pathways, it was nothing more than a memory. The countertop had been wiped enough times to fade the red, and while the old-style stools were stable-looking, I preferred the safety of a table.

That is where I put my foot down with Taylor. I did not want to find myself sitting on the ground, with everyone laughing at me. But after counting the number of empty stools, we would have been better off skipping the table.

We had barely settled in when the waitress came over with a pair of water glasses and a solo shot of orange juice. From the smile she beamed at Taylor, I figured the girls were at least semi-regulars. And Taylor was well liked by the locals.

Sandy got along with the waitress, I got a questioning look, which gave off neither cold nor heat, which my granddaughter noticed and answered.

"Mel!" Taylor grabbed up the waitress's hand. "You got to be nice to him. He's my granpa."

"Then he must be nice."

"Most of the time." Taylor dragged over a booster seat and placed it on the chair closest to the orange juice. "He made my mommy cry, but I don't think he meant to."

"Well, if he does it again"—Mel leaned over to give Taylor a hug—"we'll spice up his food big time."

"Before or after it is cooked?"

I meant it as joke, but Mel's expression held no humor.

"Both, I do most of the cooking for my favorite customers."

"Let me guess." I tried one last time to tease out a smile. "Mel is short for Melanie."

"I am not going to admit anything." Then the smile finally came. "But this is my place."

"And she orders for me." Taylor tugged at my attention from across the table. "Makes breakfast into a surprise party."

"Well then, I will have to let Mel ordered for me too."

Sandy added her nod as well, and Mel held up three fingers. Not smart enough to leave well enough alone, I made the big mistake of holding up a spread hand to add John and Salem to our order.

"Five?"

"Six!"

The voice announcing the added diner had a grating effect on Mel and didn't do a whole lot for my mood neither. I had only heard him speak once, but I had no trouble recognizing the voice. Without checking the mood around the rest of the table, I turned toward the door.

"Salem didn't tell me you were coming."

"Guess that makes me another breakfast surprise."

Chapter 44

MORE LIKE A BREAKFAST SPOILER, but for once, I kept my mouth shut.

Father walking in with John and Salem was not what I was expecting. It might dampen any talk about my plans for the future, but not much. I was not going to say that much in front of Taylor, and I knew Salem could be a spy.

Curling up at my feet for the night did not earn her any trust points. I was not a Mark Anthony, and Salem was no Cleopatra. But another time in my life who knows she might have made a good pet.

I shook my head, not sure where the last though had come from.

It forced me to take another look at Salem, standing submissively behind Father.

I couldn't be sure, but I felt as if I had just stumbled across some hidden truth I had been missing. It was an itch in the back of my mind that was really bothering me, but with Father here, there was no time to scratch it.

"Do you mind if I join you?"

"Not at all." But the look I gave Mel spoke more toward the truth. "Make it six of your choice."

"Excuse me, I prefer to do my own ordering." Father gave me a knowing smile as if I were his best friend. "After all, you know how the help is in these places."

Mel flashed a smile that would have melted sugar or butter if you looked past the surface to see the heat. She took Father's order without a word to any of us, and for a moment, I was not sure eating here was a good idea. I didn't care for having spit in my food, or something even worse. I might have suggested moving our meal, but Taylor grabbed at Mel's sleeve as she turned to leave.

"Mel, I still want the surprise breakfast, 'cause you're the best."

The rod slid out of Mel's back, and she patted Taylor's hand.

"Don't worry, babe. Everyone will get a very special breakfast just because of you." Mel's parting grin was friendly to all of us but the Father and Salem. They got the one reserved for rodents.

Salem started to slide into the seat on the far side of Taylor, but a muffled cough halted her mid dip. She looked to Father and backed away with her head tucked against her chin. In the end, Salem was forced into the chair between me and John. It was at a hard angle from Taylor and directly down the long length of the table from Father.

I felt the hand reaching for mine and turned back to Father. His reaching movement had barely started, but Taylor's was already shrinking my way. When he saw me turning to face him, Father halted his reach, and the creepy crawling on the back of my hand stopped.

"Tell me, Mr. Grandfather . . ." Father's use of the title turned it into something cheap. "What are your plans for my little girl?"

"Not sure that is something I want to talk about."

"Come now." Father stared me straight in the eyes with more dare than Santa had ever served up. "I have helped take care of Sandy and Taylor for the last few years. Surely, you can grant me some interest in the child."

"Well, my first interest is to help Sandy get a job."

"I already helped with that." Father closed his hands together in a tent and looked to Sandy with an ingratiating smile or to my eyes a smirk. "I have directed several of the ladies to her with house cleaning jobs."

"I was thinking more of a job with steady hours, pay, and benefits." I watched for a flicker of annoyance behind Father's Santa Claus smile. "Something you can raise a child on."

"We're a small town and do not have many good jobs like that around here." Father's hand tent grew taller as it came up to his mouth. "But I am sure we will find one eventually."

"*Eventually* doesn't feed the child."

"I have always made sure the child was fed." Father caught Sandy's uncomfortable squirm out of the corner of his eye. "And I will be here for Sandy as well."

I could feel the heat of my temper beginning to head toward a slow boil when I felt a leg rub up against mine. At first, I figured it might be John stretching out but quickly realized the leg was coming from an angle to my side and was much smaller.

It had to be Salem, and this was one hell of a time to flirt with me. I was three times her age. She could do better, and I was about to have a confrontation with Father. I could already feel the lift in my blood pressure and, from past experience, knew it headed toward the old oil rig gusher mode.

Elder or not, I was going to make Father listen. But this time, as I straighten up full height in my chair to address the man, the leg rub got firmer and the foot at its end gave me an ankle kick.

In spite of myself, I looked away from the Father and turned in Salem's direction. It was then I caught on to the meaning of the leg rubbing and grabbed out for something to say.

"What do you think, Salem?"

That's it, dummy. Put Salem right in the middle. I am sure she will appreciate the move, especially while she seems to be trying hard to keep me from putting my foot in mouth. A move I have become famous for at times.

"Father is a wise old man. I am sure he keeps the best interest of Sandy and Taylor foremost in his mind at all times."

"Child, you are too kind."

I couldn't have said it better myself, but I would have been serious. Even the tone was good. With comments like that, Salem should be teaching butt-kissing 201 or at least getting an A+ from the teacher.

"I care equally about all my children." Father's tented fingers moved down away from his mouth to take a spread position to either side of his place setting. "So what are your plans for my girls?"

"Granpa is going to take care of me." Taylor quit sipping at her orange juice and plunked the empty glass down between us. "He'll take us someplace else, where Mommy and I can see him all the time."

"He is?" The fingers on the right side of Father's place mat clenched like the tightening of a throttling. "And when is all this going to happen."

"Soon." Hackles up, Taylor turned to me. "Right, Granpa?"

My smile was probably a safe enough confirmation, but I wanted to say something more. Still, I had to be careful. I did not want to tell a lie, which would come back later to haunt me, probably about the time when I got ready to go home.

I should have told the lie.

Father had no such reservations. He could go for the throat and didn't mind hurting people.

"But you would have to leave Salem!"

"Nooo!" Hackles and voice went up further. "She will come with us."

"Are you leaving me, Salem?"

"I haven't been asked."

"Ask her Granpa!"

"Now is not the time." My granddaughter's face caved in with shock, and the pressure of Salem's leg went away. "I haven't thought any further ahead than tomorrow."

"And what is tomorrow."

"Another trip to McDonald's and some clothes shopping for Sandy and Taylor." I swallowed hard to avoid punching the old man in the face as his ugly smirk grew larger, and my granddaughter sank further into her seat.

"Going to use your Ranger?"

"Your car, with your permission, of course."

"Just make sure you bring it back."

"Your car?"

"Taylor, my little girl."

Chapter 45

BEFORE OUR CONVERSATION COULD GO any further, Mel came back with the first of our surprises.

Taylor was served first with a giggling producing flourish, but no one complained. Instead we all joined in with the giggling except for Father. He allowed himself nothing but a mirthless smile.

But that was his problem. I was just happy to see a smile back on Taylor's face.

The rest of our orders were right behind Taylor's, with each of us being served a different dish in turn. John got a plate heaped with everything, but a side order of ice cream and that might have been hidden at the bottom of the plate while Sandy was favored with a trio of poached eyes nestled in rye toast. Salem got some lean meat swimming in rich gravy, better looking than any I have ever seen before.

While mine had pancakes so full of blueberries, I couldn't take a bite without getting the rich taste of them in my mouth, and syrup was not really needed. It was the only plate matching another at the table.

"Granpa, we got the same thing."

"Means we're two of a kind."

"No, I'm a girl." Taylor wrinkled her nose at me. "You're a boy."

Hard to argue with Taylor's logic, and I was learning better than to try. Made more sense to ask Taylor why she thought we got the same dish. And she gave me her answer without hesitation.

"Because Mel likes us the best."

Guess that meant Mel didn't like Father at all.

His meal came last and not exactly the way he had order it.

The sunny-side-up eggs with a hard yolk came as a running white mess one step above raw. The crispy bacon had been crisped to a blackened mess with the toast looking unheated. I am not sure about Father's coffee, but I would not have touched it on general principles.

Father seemed to ignore the condition of his plate and nodded an "Everything is all right" to Mel's inquiry about how our meals were. Only those looking closely at Father's face would have seen the "I will get even" smolder in the depths of Father's eyes.

"Separate checks?"

"Father, are you treating us to breakfast?"

Salem's leg movement was a clawing this time, with the foot kick almost sending me into a start. It halted my own offer to pay before it was uttered, and Father answered almost at once.

"Of course, and Salem." Father's smile would have frozen a mountain lion's charge mid leap. "Make sure you add a gracious tip. I would not want to have our wonderful service going unnoticed."

Mel gave the table an evil smile and totaled up the bill. When done, she slapped it in front of Father with a bull fighting flourish. He pushed it down the table toward Salem not even close to within her reach.

I reached out with a finger and hesitated before passing it down.

"Father does not carry money, and I handle his finical business."

Such as paying bills and controlling the money. That gave Salem a very vested interest in Father's welfare and reminded me to back off on the trust level. Girls as attractive as Salem often caused a letdown of barriers, usually with disastrous results. I had a little charmer of my own here, and could not afford such results.

"You have made a mistake. There are only five breakfasts listed on here."

Mel waved away Salem's efforts to hand the tab back and placed the hand firmly on her hip closest to Father. "I will not allow him to pay for my little angel."

"Me!"

Taylor looked up at Mel with a blueberry-smeared smile.

"Of course." Mel pinched at Taylor cheek and somehow avoided a blueberry staining of her own fingers. "I am sure no one else at this table comes close to qualifying, including your humble servant."

Father's expression said elsewise, at least in his mind. With a faltering of his smile, Father got to his feet and motioned for Salem to follow. In response, Salem came out of her chair, digging into the right hand pocket of the jeans. The hand came out with a money clip containing more than enough to pay for breakfast, and I wondered if all of Father's bills were paid in cash.

As Salem was dropping several of the bills on the table, Father turned his back on us. But before Father got to the door, he twisted around to throw a parting command in my direction.

"Remember, I am very protective of what is mine."

I doubt if Father remained looking at us long enough to see my one-finger answer. John chuckled in agreement, and Mel beamed two degrees brighter than the sun. But Sandy was not impressed as she stared at her daughter's reaction.

"Granpa!"

Taylor's shock was even more apparent on her face. It left me feeling like a naked guy at the Super Bowl who just realized halfway across the field that there was no way out. To say I wanted to crawl under the table was an understatement.

"It's okay, your grandfather just wanted to point out the door to Father and accidently used the wrong finger."

"Salem!" At least Taylor's attention was off me. "I'm six and not still a baby."

"That you are." Salem leaned past me to kiss Taylor's cheek.

Probably in an innocent movement, but it brought her upper body across the back of my head and stirred old memories, which were not innocent. It would have helped a lot if Salem was built more like Mel and less like a slinky slimmed-down playmate. My mind slammed past lust so hard I almost missed the second part of her comment to Taylor.

"But sometimes I wish you had stayed the baby."

Salem straightened up with a second brushing and made to follow Father while exchanging verbal partings with everyone but me and Taylor. Taylor was graced with a second kiss, blown instead of lip delivered, and me?

I got a look.

There is no way to describe such a look, but every man beyond the age of puberty understands it. You have to, because it reaches into your gut and drags out your most primitive memories. It was like a reliving of caveman 101, and it took everything I had not to come out of the chair and beat my chest.

Of course, being sixty-two might have helped to slow any such reaction. That and the fact I had an eagle-eyed six-year-old sitting at my elbow. A chest beating would have been hard to explain. Speaking of which, I turned to John.

"How did you end up bringing Father along?"

"Didn't have much of a choice." John shoveled in a final bit of egg and bacon wrapped in toast and then chewed a couple of times before finishing. "Father was in tow when Salem showed up."

Well, that shriveled up the lust and pushed Salem back into the bad-guy camp.

I guess we can't always get our wishes.

Of course it would be nice if I could get just one wish granted.

Chapter 46

PLANS FOR AFTER BREAKFAST HAD been limited to begin with, and now?

Sandy thought she should check on her tomorrow cleaning jobs. She needed to clear up time for our shopping trip without losing money. John suggested a movie, if we could find one age right for Taylor.

For once, Taylor had no ideas, and me?

I just wanted to go home and forget this whole trip.

I was too old and tired to be influencing other people lives. Helping people should be left to those who knew better than to lose their son on a foreign battlefield. A wise father would have found a way to protect his boy, or at least learn to stay out of other people's business.

Not me, I came out here and made things worse for them. So far, I had offered them a false hope, upset Sandy's working status, and lusted after a girl perhaps a third of my age. That had to make me a work of art, a poor work.

"Granpa . . ." The hand grasping at mine dragged me back to reality away from my pouting. "Are you still going to leave us?"

"Taylor, I am getting you out of here." I rolled my fingers to take her hand in mine. "But I don't think I am taking you back home with me."

"You don't want me?"

"I don't know if I am the best option for you."

Taylor chewed at her lip, and I search for a word to use instead of option. But I found Taylor's hesitation was from thinking and not misunderstanding.

"But you might be."

I started to go over my feelings to explain the situation, but I felt a second being, not in body but spirit or memory. It originated during a conversation shortly before Junior's death. He had called during a late-night lull and for some reason just before he had to get off made a switch of subject comment, which I never got a chance to follow up. I had pushed it into the background since Junior's death until Sandy's reminder had brought it back to the surface.

And now the words rose from his grave.

"You know I want to have lots of kids, old man. What you also need to know is I am going to be the same type of father you were."

"I remembered; back into the depth of Junior's blue eyes, in a young recreation."

"Yep, I might be."

Chapter 47

A S PER USUAL WITH LADIES, our Miss Taylor had a sudden attack of "I need a restroom." I volunteered to be the escort, but thankfully, Sandy stepped in. With a mother's smile, she followed the wiggling six-year-old back into the restaurant.

I stayed outside and looked at the graying sky.

"The rain is not forecasted to be here before tomorrow night at the earliest."

I looked back over my shoulder to see Mel leaning against the restaurant front with a cigarette dangling from her fingers. She held it up for me to see but took no puff before dropping her hand back to her side. I focused on the twirl of smoke until it disappeared and then shuffled back to lean besides Mel.

"The forecaster ever wrong?"

"Are yours?"

"Only during the spring, summer, fall, and winter seasons."

"Sounds like we have the same weatherman." Mel brought the cigarette up to her face but again did not smoke it. "Except half the time ours is a lady."

"Same here." We exchanged a smile before I broached the question hanging in the wind. "Seems like not too many people around here like the Father."

"Less than you think."

I stopped for a moment to chew at something in the back of my mouth. It could have been a blueberry skin or just my imagination. And it kept me from asking the one question I had to, but did not want an answer for.

"Why does Father stick around?"

"Because he wants to."

"And people like his money?"

"We are a dying town stuck in the last century." Mel again made a move to bring her cigarette up but stopped way short of her face. "The young kids are leaving for better jobs, and nobody is moving in. Give us a few more generations, and there will not be a town."

"Can't you bring in some tourists?"

"I think Father discourages that from happening."

"And the people in town put up with it?"

"People in this town are afraid of Father." Mel flicked the cigarette toward the street, bouncing the stub twice across the sidewalk before it settled into the gutter still glowing. "I'm afraid of Father."

"You didn't look it when serving us breakfast."

"Taylor is a special little lady, and she reminds me of my own daughter before I lost her to a better future in Pittsburg." Mel took a yearning look at the curb. "I had to keep Father's attention off Taylor."

"Why?" I pushed away from the wall and flung my arms out to either side. "What can he do?"

"I don't know, and I don't want to find out."

Mel spun away from me, maybe realizing she had said too much. I thought she was going to leave, but she held back.

"You love your granddaughter."

"I think so."

"Then don't go back home without getting Taylor out of here."

"Why?"

"Because bad things happen when the witch's rose comes back to town, and I think I saw one last night."

Chapter 48

MEL TURNED AWAY, AND THE lady's return kept me from chasing after her. Then before I could make up an excuse to go back in the restaurant, John pulled up with my Ranger and popped open the door.

"Time to get Sandy to work." John grinned across at me like a little boy playing hooky. A look I seldom saw with the veterans of my son's unit. "Do you mind if I stick with her and help."

"Would it do any good if I did?"

Both of them smile an answer at me, and I gathered up my granddaughter in an attempt to make a face-saving retreat.

"We'll be at the park or ice-cream place if it begins to rain." Taylor's face swiveled up to look at me, and I met her question with a stage whisper. "Or even if it doesn't rain, but we won't tell them about it."

Taylor grinned and waved me down to whisper into my ear.

"Why not?"

"Because I think they are going to get a taste of their own sweets."

Taylor gave me a puzzled look but lost it quickly as she turned to wave goodbye at the departing couple. We make for the park in Father's loaner, but only after a quick ice-cream stop on the way.

We found some other children enjoying the park, including Taylor's best friend from school. They greeted each other with little girl hugs and started off to the swings with an arm around each other's shoulders. They were apparently going to exchange reports on the summer happenings in their lives, and by the way their arms were going through the air, a large dose of kiddie gossip was also on the menu.

"Even grandfathers come in second place to friends at Taylor's age."

"Best friend only."

Even without knowing the voice, I would have realized it was Salem behind me. Her chest pressing against the back of my head had been a dead giveaway and came about the same times as her words. It did wonders for my cardiac acceleration, and I had to remind myself of Salem's standing in our situation to avoid showing my excitement.

Would have been easier if Salem was uglier than sin.

"Well then, I guess it is okay." Salem plunked herself down next to me on the bench I had chosen. "And of course, they have to put some distance between you."

"Why?"

"Because, Grandpa, you are undoubtedly the main topic of the conversation."

"You think so?" I grinned in spite of my effort for control.

"I know so." Salem's hand reached out to pat at my lower thigh. "I figure you have been the topic of a lot of girlie chats."

"I am too old for that."

"Real men are never too old." Salem reached out to rotate my head toward her, forcing me to look into her misshaped eyes. "And you are a real man."

I thought of a million arguments against such a status, but none of them would fly in the face of Salem's look. It was as if she had taken the last few days to evaluate me beyond the surface to the inner depths of my being.

I wasn't sure if I wanted to know Salem's conclusions.

"I am too old for you."

Salem actually mewed out a smile that would have fitted perfectly on a cat about to eat the canary. I found myself breaking out one of my own in spite of the topic.

"Age gap can be a problem." Salem's smile widened beyond cat to a very human "I know something you don't. And you may have miscalculated our age gap."

"Not that much." I dragged my eyes away from her to look after Taylor and avoid becoming more lost in Salem's eyes. "And I would not feel right taking advantage of you."

"It might be me taking advantage of you."

Maybe, but not in the way I was talking about.

Salem was Father's tool, and using a young girl's body against an old man's foolishness would not be anything new. Even knowing this, it was hard for me to remain in control.

"Maybe neither one of us should be taking advantage of the other."

Great statement, but it would have worked better if I had not looked back into Salem's face. It was filled with both an amusement and an intense sexuality. I actually felt myself leaning into her, and I have to think a kiss was coming.

But at the last moment, I was rescued by Mel's little angel.

"Granpa!"

Chapter 49

I GOT TO MEET MELISSA, A somewhat heavier version of Taylor. She had a rounded face and brown ringlets that reminded me of Shirley Temple. The girls had gone to school together last year, and both were experts on the good and bad of kindergarten. A subject they were willing to discuss with me for the better part of an hour.

Of course, the conversation could have been a little show and tell for Taylor. With Sandy having to work, Taylor did not get much of a chance to exhibit a family, and I could see where Taylor might be taking advantage of my presence.

To tell the truth, it made me feel kind of special. I hadn't become old hat to my other granddaughters, but at the same time, I was not the new toy in the box.

Their chatting might have gone on for a lot longer, but Melissa's mother gave out a call from across park bench as she prepared to leave. So with a goodbye hug and a promise of seeing Taylor soon in school, Melissa was off.

"Want me to play?"

"No." Taylor gave out with a sigh not much different than Junior's. "I'm kind of tired and want to sit here next to Granpa."

"Guess I have been replaced." Salem gave me a wink out of Taylor's sight line. "By an older man no less."

"Don't be sad, Salem." Taylor came across with a tone of voice older than mine. "I will play with you next time after Granpa has gone home."

Salem went silence.

All sense of play left Salem's face, and she curled both legs up on to the bench. Then without meeting my eyes, she made a pillow of her interlocked hands and placed them on my shoulder. Suddenly, I had become a sleeping post with two heads using me as a pillow. Taylor's tucked up into my upper rib cage on the left while Salem's rested on my other arm just short of my shoulder.

Together, we must have made quite a family picture, the child, the youthful mother, and the old grandfather. All we needed was a father figured to make it perfect. And since we were using Salem as a stand-in mother, we could have used John as the father.

Then I felt the heads to either side slipping into matching measured breathing.

I folded my left arm around Taylor and edged the right hand out against Salem hip. With everything now in place, I closed my own eyes. Beneath their closure, I could make a more picture perfect.

All I had to do was add Junior.

Chapter 50

A COUPLE OF HOURS LATER, JOHN found us in the same position minus Salem. Apparently, she had made her escape under the cover of my snoring. Knowing how loud I snored, I didn't blame her.

"Sandy, even with my help, is whipped out." John plunked himself down while Taylor rubbed the sleep out of her eyes. "I fed Sandy a snack and dropped her off at the house for a nap."

"And us?"

"We still have time for a refuel at Mel's and the seven-o'clock movie."

"Movie?"

How is it that a six-year-old barely dragging herself awake one second can burst forth like a chirping morning bird the next, all caused by the simple utterance of the single word *movie*?

The rest of the day slid by with the pace of an old-time black-and-white movie. It would not have surprised me if a band had jumped out at us with Judy Garland belting out a version of "Somewhere over the rainbow."

Instead, I got a shadow meal at Mel's.

It seems like there was something missing. The steak was better than most, and with Taylor at our table, the service was two steps above average. The only thing I could think of was our host. Not sure if Mel's absence was the total cause for the invasion of bland, but it was definitely a contributing factor.

The movie was a more fast-paced, with granpa making several trips to the refreshment stand for a six-year-old taking advantage of the absence of her mother. By the time we had finished the movie,

Taylor was feeling less than peppy with a lot of stomach rubbing and a few groans.

Luckily, Taylor made us stop on the way home, long enough to get rid of most of the movie treats. Usually, I would have considered this a bad thing, but a sleepy kid was easier to sneak past an irate mother than one heaving her guts out.

But not by much.

Sandy greeted us at the door in a bathrobe and frown.

"Let me guess." Sandy swinging the door out and coming out on the porch was not real encouraging. "Taylor got you with the 'I'm hungry, and I never get any treats gambit.'"

"Taylor didn't exactly say never."

"Did she have to?"

I hunched my shoulder to one side, and Sandy got her answer. But instead of lashing into me, Sandy came down the steps and ruffled Taylor hair.

"Young lady, you owe your granpa an 'I'm sorry.'"

Taylor looked up at me with a face full of anguish. I could tell it was real, but I was not sure if the pain came from the heart, stomach, or most likely both. She tried to work up the words "I'm sorry" but just moved the lips silently.

"Hey, kid, do you want a hug?"

Taylor half nodded and then was in my arms. She held on to my neck with a very uncomfortable death grip, yet I would not have loosened it for all the air in the world.

"Granpa." Taylor rubbed her head into my face to get close to my ear. "I don't feel very good."

"Too many treats?"

"Maybe" was Taylor's verbal answer, but her head scrapping a nod on the side of my face felt more truthful. "Can I go to bed?"

I look over at Sandy, and she nodded.

With a groan, I came to my feet with Taylor still clinging to my neck. Either the lift or the angle of cling was wrong, and I felt an old pull in my back. It hadn't bothered me in a long time, but the long-remembered pain came back full force.

John saw the look on my face and stepped over to take Taylor from me. At first, I resisted, but a second and third jolt of pain running up my back and then down my leg convinced me otherwise. I could have handled carrying Taylor inside, but I would have paid for it the next day. The pain of handing Taylor off to John made me wonder if I might be paying the price anyway.

Sandy's hand on my hip helped me lean back against the porch railing. There I was able to settle my weight into the rail enough to open my eyes. To avoid the questioning in Sandy's eyes, I looked past her shoulder at the ground.

"Sandy, do you have more of those tonight than you had last night?"

"I guess so." With a puzzled look, Sandy checked both sides of the porch. "Maybe they get thicker as the summer goes along."

"When did you plant them?"

"I didn't." Sandy looked around again as if making a rough count of the blossoms coming out. "They just sort of grew."

"But they don't grow in your neighbors' yards."

Sandy looked to either side of her house and across the street. "Never noticed that before."

"Where have you noticed the flowers?"

Sandy rubbed at her neck with a thumb and forefinger. Even in the dull light of the porch bulb, I could see Sandy's mind leaving me for a moment to think. It was a full two minutes before she came back to me.

"The only places I can think of are a couple of the homes where I clean house." Sandy's hand lowered down her chest. "They're both places where Father got me the job."

I looked at the fragile little flowers on my side of the porch.

"They didn't look as cute now."

Chapter 51

I DROVE BACK TO THE INN in a roundabout way checking for the flowers.

I found some scattered around the cemetery and got out to check them.

I couldn't get very close because of a rather high fence with metal points on top. I could have tried the entrance, but it was guarded by a black iron gate locked with a massive lock from the knights and castle days. It didn't look rusted out, and I doubt if John could have broken it with anything less than a couple of large chunks of concrete.

From what I could see through the fence, the flowers seemed to be patched up in clumps around several of the smaller headstones. In the dim glow of the streetlights, I could not make out any names or dates, but from the sidewalk they looked childlike, but who knew? This town was far from normal, and there could be a million reasons why the flowers clung to the smaller stones.

I drove past Father's place of worship and saw flowers around the base of the building. They were showing all the way down the length of the building and in full bloom tonight. They were lovely little flowers and made a great highlight for the other surprise of my drive.

Unlike last night, during my early evening visit inside the building, tonight all the lights were on. It emitted light up into the air like a circus, and I had to wonder if the glow was being tracked from outer space. I spared a single thought wondering if the door was again unlocked, but I made no move to slow down or follow up on my wondering.

It just seemed like a good idea to ignore things at the moment.

Wonder what I would have found if I had stopped. I didn't find much more driving around town. There was one house close to the playground, which might have been one of Sandy's cleaning jobs. But all the rest of the town I drove through was normal.

Or at least as normal as a dying town could be.

Mel's words not mine.

To me, the town looked more frozen than dying. I found no boarded-up windows or over grown yards in need of a cutting. But at the same time, I found no new construction. There might have been some inner upgrading, but not one sign advertising remodel work or a new roof going on. Like I had thought earlier in this drive, the village was going neither forward or back.

Back at the inn, I noticed the second odd ball of the night.

When I parked my truck, I took a minute to gather myself. I should have gotten out and went directly to my room, but I had to look over toward the swimming pool area down a few rooms from mine.

It wasn't much of a pool, but it did have some nice garden arrangements built up around the outside. They were blocked out into nice little squares. With the darkness, they were empty of blooms, except for the one nearest my room.

It had a multitude of little white blooms with crimson trimming showing up nicely in the inn's parking lots lights. Their presence probably didn't mean much, but by any chance was the witch rose a calling card from my friend the Father?

It was not one of his best ideas.

Chapter 52

I DIDN'T GET UP TO ANY rain, but you could not blame the sky. The clouds were dark beyond gray, needing only a stage or two to reaching black. I felt like a bug crawling under a faucet, hoping to make it to safety before the farmer turned on the flow.

Walking past the pool, I tried to look the other way. I knew the flowers would disappear in the light of the day, but what about the dark of overcast.

Did I really want to know?

Probably not, but I looked anyway.

I honestly made an effort to avoid it, but as I slipped into the driver seat, the pool area came into view. A moment later, I was half into the Ranger, staring at the flower box.

Maybe not quite as many as last night, but you could not miss the blooms. They were all over the box, taking over what the other flowers should have owned or at least shared.

For a long pause, I could not take my eyes off the blossoms.

They were tiny, fragile, and the loveliest flowers I had ever seen. So why did they give me the creeps?

I shook off the ice like shiver sliding down my spine and finished climbing into the Ranger. It took me a while to gather my bearings, but once out of the parking lot, I was all right and headed toward Sandy's.

Good thing I was back to normal, because coming around the corner to my granddaughter's street, I had to make a quick brake and twist to avoid a gray shadow. It looked like a large silver cat, but in the overcast light, I did not get a conclusive look.

Being truthful, I did not get much of a look at all and was mostly glad not to hear the heartbreaking thump I expected. Who knows, maybe the shadow was just my imagination. It had been stretched pretty far, further than ever before.

But back to reality, I pulled up in front of the house to find Sandy and John waiting on the porch. Neither was over happy about the looks of the sky or my arrival. I am not sure which, but I was hoping for the weather.

"Pops, glad to see you." John shuffled down the steps, and his twisted smile said otherwise.

"Is something wrong with the trip?"

"No, of course not." John looked back over his shoulder at Sandy. "Well, maybe one a little thing."

"Nobody wants to go?"

John gave me a "you got to be kidding" look.

"Taylor wants to go, so we all want to go."

"Even Salem." Sandy's add on came out as a whisper. I think Sandy was hoping for a miss on my part, but she was out of luck.

"You asked her to come?"

"She showed up with breakfast and asked about our day." John spread his hands. "What else could I do?"

Kept his mouth shut, but it was too late for that. Besides, I am not sure if I was pissed or happy. After all, if Salem was with us, she could not be up to anything. Well, at least nothing out of our sight.

"Okay." I nodded to John. "Better get the girls so we can be back before the downpour."

About then, Taylor came out of the house, sipping on the last of a juice carton. "I'm ready."

"Where is Salem?"

"She left." Taylor finished the juice with a long draw, continuing after the carton was empty to set off a very noisy slurp. "Had to do kiddie business for Father."

"But how did Salem get past us?" Sandy's question beat mine by half a heartbeat.

"She went out the back."

"And what went over the fence?"

"I don't think so, but she was in her kiddie form."

Not sure what that meant and was not sure I wanted to know. I was just hoping kiddie was the correct word for Salem's business. The way this visit was going, anything seemed possible.

At least I could feel some relief about our trip to the next town. There might have been a little disappointment mixed in, but if so, it must have come from my lack of common sense.

Of course, John and Sandy had to confirm the announcement and set off to check it out. Taylor rolled her eyes at me and continued as if they were still here.

"Salem promised she would catch up with us later." Great, so much for relief. Made all the better when Taylor added her convictions. "And she will be there, 'cause Salem always keeps her promises to me."

That finished it. My emotions bounced back to their original fight between hope and terror.

Either way, I figured I was going to end up a loser.

Chapter 53

OUR DAY OF SHOPPING TOOK a lot longer than planned. My accidental over sleep had not helped the start, and like the weather, everything seemed to crawl forward dark and foreboding. At times during the ride, I almost prayed for the plunk of a fat, pregnant drop of rain. I needed it to explode across our windshield with the flaming energy of Grecian fire and burn my tension down to a reasonable level.

But I got nothing, not even the relief of a misting.

Lunch was a Bob Evans selection of sandwiches and soups. And after eating one too many meals at the inn, it felt like a banquet of exotic delight. The shopping was less so.

Taylor had never been promised three full outfits for the start of school before. She used this promise to try on a dozen outfits in every one of the girl friendly shops located in the Bob Evans hostess recommend mall.

Any other time, I would have faked the excitement of a real interest. My mind was so full of white flowers, a dying city, and a girl I did not want to know more about, that it was hard to filter in the joy of Taylor's fervor.

Or it was until we reached the last shop.

"Well, missy, which outfits do you want?"

"None of them." Taylor's answer to Sandy's question caught us all off guard.

"You didn't like any of them?"

"I liked most of them." Taylor tucked herself up on a rest bench and looked to me. "Granpa did not like any of them."

"Excuse me!"

"You did not look at most of them, and you never smiled."

I closed my eyes and forced away the interfering thoughts. It took me a few moments, and when I opened my eyes, I had to wave myself through the defensive flak being put up by John and Sandy.

"I am not the best guy for picking out little girl's clothes."

"Most daddies and granpas aren't." Taylor tilted her head to the right and gave me the understand look of an educated six-year-old. "I learned that from the other girls in school."

"But I should have shown more interest."

Taylor nodded. "And you were sad-looking. I don't want you to be sad from spending too much money on me."

"Never going to happen." I went down on one knee and brushed some hair back from her forehead. "At least not until you turn sixteen."

Taylor smiled and reached up to press my hand against her cheek. "I love you, Granpa."

"Me too."

"It's good when we both love you."

I started to correct Taylor and realized she was right to a degree. Around her, it was getting easier to put away the "what ifs" and think more about the "what might be."

"Okay, but it is getting late, kid."

"I know." Taylor kissed my hand and let it go as she prepared to shove herself off the bench. "But I don't need the clothes that bad."

"Sure you do, and here are the conditions."

I gave Taylor a nudge to the back of the bench and put my eyes within twelve inches of hers and then counted the conditions off on my fingers.

"One, you will pick out three stores."

"Two, you and I will go back to those stores."

"Three, you and I will pick out one outfit from each of those stores."

"And four, you will have to go through the school year with the results of my poor taste."

Taylor's smile got bigger with each condition and got downright giggly with the fourth. She pushed off the bench and into my arms.

Without further hesitation, I started back into the depths of a hell called the mall.

When Sandy and John made to follow us, I stopped them.

"You two go the other way." I jabbed my finger toward the food court part of the mall. "Buy yourself something to eat, or find me a *Doctor Who* episode 88 or 91. I am still missing those."

Sandy looked at me like I was out of my mind while John tried to explain about *Doctor Who*. She stayed confused but followed John.

An hour later, we met back at the food court. They each had a new pair of jeans and a copy of *Doctor Who* number 88. Me, I had a happy Taylor, who only got to revisit two of the stores but boasted four new outfits. It was later than we liked, but everyone was feeling good, and the only thing left on my to-do list was a phone call to one of my loving twins.

I didn't even care which twin.

I had pretty well made up my mind on our next course of action, and finding out about Father's so-called church did not matter.

Or so I thought.

My baby girl dashed that with the first sentence.

Chapter 54

"**D**ADDY, I THINK WE FOUND what you were looking for."

"Information about the Church of Our Father." I started to tell her to forget it, but my younger twin had never been one for slow conversation.

"Wrong word, Dad." I heard the ruffle of paper in the background and knew she was arranging notes. She never needed notes but kept them close like a security blanket. Drove her sister crazy at times, but I think that might have been part of the reason she took notes.

"Cult of Our Father."

"Worse!" I heard the deep breath, held in for a gushing answer. "It is not a church or cult, but a coven."

"A what?"

"A coven of witches and a rather strange coven at that."

"There is such a thing as a normal coven?" Even as I uttered it, I knew the comment was stupid, but I was tugging for a balance I couldn't grasp. It seemed to hang in the air just beyond my reach.

And baby girl was not done pushing the balance further away yet.

"Compared to these guys, everything else about witchcraft is as normal as blueberry pies." Only the older twin liked apples; my baby girl hardly admitted they existed. At the moment, I wished she had felt the same way about witchcraft.

At least I didn't have to ask in what way. Baby girl was not one to slow down when on a roll.

"The Coven of Our Father is an all-male coven, and they have been around off and on for over two hundred years." With a pause, which might have actually been a note check, I got a chance to let the words sink in partway, but then she continued. "I have half a dozen pages of things they were accused of, none of them nice."

"Any with kids."

"Just girls, something about life extension."

"How young?"

"Pre-puberty."

"Like six?"

"More like eight or ten, but the information is sketchy." The gush slowed suddenly as if she saw where we were going. "Do you want me to look for more?"

"Not really, you gave me the answer I needed."

"Daddy, come home."

"I will be heading home tomorrow, just as soon as I can get everyone packed."

"Daddy, forget everyone else and get out now."

"Baby girl!" I used my hold-on tone and waited a pair of heart-beats to make sure she was listening. "Do you really expect me to do that?"

"No, but you should."

"I will be out of here first thing in the morning with everyone important coming along."

"Daddy?"

"Yes."

"If I don't hear from you by the end of work tomorrow, sis and I are coming after you." The words were coming hard, but she had to end them with the family humor. "With the kids, and I'm sickin' them on you the whole way back home."

"I love you too."

We hung up mutually, and I looked over to my other family getting ready to leave. It was than the downpour let go, and my walk over to the car became a dash and dive for the passenger seat.

I didn't get soaked beyond dampness, but the rain gave me another reason for packing up on the morrow instead of tonight. I did not want to fight both the dark and the rain when clearing out the girl's clothes into the back of my Ranger.

And that was my last though on the subject until we reached the turn off to go back. At that corner, I reached out and grabbed John's shirt sleeve for a second, earning me a questioning look from the big guy.

I thought about directing him to Pittsburg but shrugged and released John's arm instead. After all, Father had not made any real threats, and John's size was a big stopper of action.

Still, the one word did bother me.

Pre-puberty was not an exact age.

Chapter 55

I EXPECTED THE RAIN TO LET up.

Even if God was flushing out his entire sewer system, the downpour could only stay full force for a few minutes at best.

Boy was I the weather wizard. Not only did a steady stream of huge, fat droplets continue to fall, they speeded up the pace. Even on high, the window wipers were barely opening a peephole with each swipe, which was gone long before the return stroke.

In the end, that was probably a good thing, at least for Salem.

If John had been going even twenty miles an hour, he would have taken her out without being able to touch his brakes. As it was, Salem only cleared the driver's fender by making a quick side hop away from our skidding car.

At first, I figured with the stream-like rain coating the pavement, we were going to skid into a rock wall. But I quickly realized we were in one of the many gaps between the cutout sections. Our crash and burn was replaced by a hard slide into the graveled shoulder of the road.

Once we came to a full stop, I turned to check on the girls, but Salem was already ripping their door open. She was tugging at the seat belt holding Taylor's car seat in place and yelling at Sandy.

"Hurry up, we got to get off the road."

Sandy flipped open her belt and started reacting without thinking. I tried to slow it down.

"Why?"

"Father is following you." A tug was bringing Taylor up from her seat before I could ask my next question Salem was already answering. "His sons have the road blocked up in front of you."

"Hold on."

Too late, Taylor was out the door, and Sandy was following. John was making an exit to follow Sandy, and I was not letting Taylor out of my sight. A glance told me the car was completely off the roadway. Not that it mattered; I was already pushing up the hillside after Taylor.

By the fourth step, I felt the nerve in my back quiver with the memory of old pain. A few more steps took the jolts of throbbing beyond anything remembered and into a brand-new landscape of misery. It was about then I reached for hidden reserves, trusting on buried character and pride to keep me going.

They did, but the hand reaching back over my shoulder and into my armpit did not hurt the effort. With arms full, Salem still had enough going to help my ascent up the hillside while vocally encouraging Sandy and John at the same time.

Crossing skinny little Salem in a battle no longer looked so approachable. I could only be glad she was on our side, or so I hoped.

The hillside's incline shot up to thirty degree as we left the road-way and felt like sixty with the rain falling and undergrowth slick vines and flowers. But at least the rain seemed to be letting up to a downfall instead of torrent. Not sure Sandy, even with her military training, would have made it up the hill without John's strong arm help.

And me?

Looking back, I would have probably drowned myself panting in the falling rain. But only if a heart attack had not gotten me first.

Eventually, the incline leveled out to a broken level where I was able to keep up on my own. But even then, I showed my age. Too tired to think, I made an effort to go straight ahead. Salem had to come back a few strides and tug me toward the right direction, the one taking us back the way we had just driven.

The time was late evening an hour or so before the setting of the sun, but the darkness was next to complete. Both John and I might have walked off the lip, which appeared suddenly to our right. The fall would have taken us back to the highway much quicker than our climb and with even worse results.

But again, Salem's hand reached out first to John and then me. She nodded at a point when the dark became even blacker. Both John and I whispered out a "We see" and thanked our lucky stars Sandy was on the inside of Salem where she needed no such warning.

A few more yards and Salem was again dragging us deeper into the brush on what felt like an extra-large deer trail. We twisted and turned like a group of blind bats in a wind tunnel. By the time we hit the houses, I was so confused, I would have been lucky to tell up from down, let alone north from south.

I would not have seen the houses, but the rain actually came to a halt. Not a drifting away, but an "all at once, I am all done" halt. It gave me a pause to stop and study the houses.

I didn't like what I was seeing.

Both houses were shapeless rectangles without porch or foundation showing. It might have been the dark, but the windows looked glassless, and the boards lacked any coloring I could see.

Salem led us down the near side of the closer building, confirming my first impressions and added more. The siding boards were not only without color, they were also rough-hewed, and I picked up a splinter when I ran my hand over them. That should have placed the building at newly constructed, but they were no signs of recent activity.

With the stoppage of rain, the twilight had finally peeked through. It was not bright enough to make things comfortable but did show a lack of scuffing on the ground where ladders or people hammering would have stood.

Salem hugged the wood as we glided around the corner and found an entrance within the first three steps. It held no real door barring the entrance, but the gaping hole was door shaped and the right size. I followed Salem in, having little choice at the moment.

I might have liked the situation better if Salem had brought an escape car or at least an escape route, but from what I could see, there was no drive way in or out.

Which brought us to the next question.

How had they brought the construction material in for the houses?

Chapter 56

INSIDE, THE HOUSE ONLY ASKED more questions.

The layout was in a section of squares with only one door leading in and a second leading out of each room. The rectangle shape of the house provided for three of these squares on either half. On the entrance side, the first room was completely empty except for the wind blowing through. And even it was forced to leave the rain outside.

With a window to the front and one to the side, both without glass or curtains, we had a perfect wind-tunnel effect. Therefore, with the strength of the recent torrent, you would have expected soaked floors, at least under the windowsills even if no place else, but the floor was dry.

Where it should have been wet and streaming, the floor looked barely a single degree above bone-dry, dusty. Stepping over to the windowsill, I found it was also dry, and only when I reached out to touch the frame on the outside of the window did I find any moisture.

I started to cross over to the other window, but John gave me a questioning look. I started to say something but realized the girls were going deeper into the house. I didn't like it but had to agree there was nothing in this room to help us.

The second room also had a single entrance and exit. It had a little more in the way of detail, with some scraping on the floor where a heavy table might have been moved. But otherwise, it was as characterless as the first, with a single rain-free window on the outer wall.

We hurried on into a third, which differed from the first two in almost every way. It did have the same window situation as first room, but it could be identified as a kitchen.

Not in today's standards, but one from a distant day before electricity became king. There was no refrigerator or even an ice box from my mother's childhood, but just an old wood burner set on a metal plate. I figured the plate, and upturned edges were there to prevent falling sparks from sending the house up in flames.

A modern stove might have worked better.

The only other things in the kitchen was a bench with a long handle pump on one end to bring up water, and a dumb waiter jutting out from the wall like a cabinet going up and down. It caught my interest the most, but Salem and the other was already leaving as I notice of the dumb waiter.

I barely checked out room 4 and 5.

Four had the table missing from room 2. No chairs, just a huge table straight out of King Arthur and the Round Table, except if you took a longer look, you realized it was more oval than round.

Room 5 fell back to the empty hole in the ground decor, with not even a dust mote in sight. It was only going into room 6, things changed in several good ways and a couple ways, which were in an undertone way, disturbing.

This room looked lived in, with a pair of mattress thrown on the floor and a number of milk cartons stacked with clothes. I counted nine shoes nestled at the foot of the bed with six of them falling into matching pairs. The inner side mattress had a trio of books scattered over the bed sheet, and all of them carried the dog-ear look of several readings. There was also a single shoe half hidden against the wall, and I was quite sure it matched one of the loners on the floor.

But there was only one doorway leading both in and out. Even with the two windows fully exposed, I felt a quiver of trap run up my spine. Throw a board or bars over the windows, and this room would make a great jail cell.

Even worse, the clothes, while mostly women's apparel, had several outfits sized too small for an adult. From where I stool, at least two of the smaller ones would have fit Taylor.

Chapter 57

"**I** DON'T LIKE IT."

Salem looked over at me as she plunked Taylor down on the outside mattress and picked up one of the two smaller outfits I had noticed. After carefully shaking out the red jeans and snowy-white shirt, Salem surveyed them before turning to Taylor.

"They'll fit, and they are dry."

"Did you hear me?"

Again, Salem acted as if I was not there. Instead, she peeled Taylor out of the wet clothes and began rubbing at her body with a discarded blouse from the nearest pile of clothing.

"Hey!" I took what I hoped was a menacing stride toward my granddaughter and Salem. "Didn't you hear me? I don't like this."

"Neither do I."

Salem snarled at me as she pivoted to face me on one knee with the other leg cocked to spring. The voice and action alone would not have stopped my charge, but the look in Salem's slotted eyes was all huntress ready to protect her young at any cost. And at that moment, I knew she would not be the one paying the cost.

Their unholy gleam was enough to arrest John as well, and he was not their target. For me, if I had been any closer, it might have stopped my heart. If nothing else, it skipped a full rotation, and my second stride not only failed to finished, it may have lost a bit of ground midair to fall back only an inch in front of the other.

"Taylor comes first, dried and dressed."

John's arm crossed my chest to grab the far shoulder and tug me back through the door. I didn't budge on the first tug, but John was a very big soldier, and his second effort overcame my stance. He added his other hand to maintain the push all the way back to the room with the big table area. There he checked my face without letting go.

"I won't kill her."

"Not sure you could." John's arms dropped. "Not sure I could."

"That was one very scary reaction."

"To hell with the look. That is one very scary little lady, period."

I looked up at John's face, and we both grinned and then giggled. The giggling brought forth a chuckle, and finally, we found ourselves in a full-out laugh. We might have stayed that way the whole night, but Sandy came out to see what was making the noise.

"Are you two crazy?"

"Are you sure you want to ask that question?" That brought forth a short chuckle from John, but more normal without the manic energy of the other laugh. "You might not like the answer."

"I've known the answer since I meant your son." Sandy came over and leaned out to put her forehead against mine. "And he was proud to be just like you."

"I don't want to spoil the moment, but I have a question for you."

We pulled away just enough to twist our faces toward John. Seeing his expression, Sandy and I both straightened up.

"How come it is dark outside?"

"John." I should have read more into his expression, but I was worn out and answered without thinking. "It gets dark outside most nights."

"But we have a nice glow in here."

"From the lights."

John's eyes dropped away from Sandy and me as a couple and focused totally on mine.

Chapter 58

"WHAT LIGHTS?"

I surveyed every part of the room.

There were no lights or holes anywhere. I even checked the floorboards, hoping maybe the lights were oozing up from an unseen basement. But there was nothing, just a glow hanging in the air and holding us in an early evening twilight.

"Maybe the wood has some type of fungus emitting the light."

"And maybe my drill instructor did not know how to yell."

"We could ask Salem." Sandy's suggestion meant with less encouragement than my fungus comment. But it did bring it to my attention Sandy's clothes were dry and different from what she had been wearing. Sandy's eyes followed my look and lifted out the bottom of her shirt about two inches with each hand.

"Salem and I are about the same size."

"So Salem keeps her clothes in two places." I looked from John to Sandy, dropping my voice still lower to prevent the words from carrying. "Neither of them home-like or very friendly."

"Depends on what you consider home-like."

Salem had a worn-out Taylor on one hip and a dirty look for the rest of us, especially me. I didn't know how much of our conversation Salem had overheard, but even the last sentence was too much.

"It is going to rain again."

"And you want to keep Taylor dry." Salem shrugged what could be either a yes, no, or "I don't give a damn." "You really think it is safe here."

"Has been for me." Salem's eyes did not meet mine, but it might have been the bouncing of her body rocking Taylor up and down.

"I think it might be safer at Sandy's."

"Father will catch you on the road." Salem began a pivot as she bounced. "And what makes you think Sandy's place is still safe."

"Father will catch us here."

"Father won't come here." The bounce did not slow, but the eyes still found mine. "He never does."

"And his friends, the local zombie squad." I was picking a fight. Not the smartest thing to do, considering I was as lost as an English preacher looking for a Japanese church in China. But I was tired and didn't care. "Do they ever come here?"

"Not very often." The bouncing stopped, and the voice rose louder. "And John can handle them if you are afraid."

"I am, but only if there are enough of them." My heart was speeding up and hitting overdrive. "And only because I am worried for Taylor's safety."

"Then forget the quiet ones and worry about Father."

"Right." I caught sight of John out of the corner on my eye. It looked like he was getting ready to hold me back or join me. But I was betting on the first. "I'm not really worried about a fat old man who looks like Santa. I'm not that bad off yet."

"Father is no Santa."

"And Father is no threat."

Salem's voice left her like the air out of balloon. If defeat was in her nature, Salem was now defeated.

"Don't worry, Salem." Taylor's head came off Salem's shoulder, blurry-eyed and exhausted. "Granpa will keep me safe."

"Taylor needed a drink."

Salem slipped past me and started toward the area of the pump handle. She was a step past the doorway before she turned back for a final whisper. "Father is a force like you have never seen before, and I hope you realize that truth before you have to face him."

I wanted to whisper "Me too" but was afraid Salem would over-hear. Nothing good could come of her knowing how deep my fears were.

Before I could worry more, John pulled me toward the window, the one facing the other house, and pointed.

Great, just what I did not want to see.

The second house had vines running all the way to the roof. All of them were flushed with the blossoms of white petals with crimson outlines.

"Father's house?"

John's question hung between us for a score of heartbeats with the words almost solid in the air. It might have remained like that forever, but I gathered myself together and added a second worse question.

"Or Salem's garden?"

Chapter 59

THE COMMENT BROUGHT JOHN'S EYES to mine and, if anything, added another cloud layer. But no words, instead he head-bobbed toward the kitchen and moved off from the window.

I followed with the intention of asking Salem if the correct answer was house or garden. That is if John did not beat me to the gun, which would be nice. I had already had my fill of fighting with Salem.

But of course, I should have known that was not going to end anytime soon.

We came through the doorway to find Taylor sandwiched between Sandy and Salem. All three were gathered around the opened dumb waiter with Taylor on her knees, staring down into it.

The wooden lip of the dumb waiter came up a foot from the floor. It wouldn't take much for a kneeling person to go over the lip and into the floor. John and I would never have fitted, and I am not sure about Sandy, leaving Salem as the only chance of following a falling Taylor.

Sandy had both her hands gripping Taylor's shoulder to keep her safe, but what I didn't like was Salem's arm around my granddaughter. I knew inside my civilized self the arm was there for safety, but what if it gave a push instead?

Perhaps sensing my thoughts, Salem turned toward me. She also tightened her grip on Taylor and turned her in our direction as well. "Your granpa wants to talk some more."

"Yeah." Forgetting the other house, I launched into my new concern. "Weren't you afraid Taylor would fall?"

"No." Salem's body did a little quiver from the neck down. "I was going to hold her feet and lower her down so she could see what was there."

I could not even get my "You were going to what?" out. All I could imagine was a bear-like yeti combination reaching up to rip my granddaughter from Salem's grip or a pool of waiting ooze bubbling below to catch my falling Taylor when Salem let go. Neither was a pleasing image, and I didn't let myself dream up a third Taylor bounced over to me with the energy of a half-deflated ball and reached up for me to take her.

"I don't want to go down there."

"You don't have to."

"She might have to."

"Over your dead body." I tighten my hold and turned Taylor away from Salem to the far hip. "And I do mean dead, if you try."

Salem started to bristle but held back while searching my face for something.

Me, I felt the old "someone's watching me" feeling. The one where you feel someone is with you but you can't turn fast enough to see or touch them. This time the feeling added a fistful of force to my last words, as if they were driven by two.

"I was not going to let Salem hold my child legs over an open hole." Sandy came between us. "I'm scare, but I am not that bad a mother."

I backed my emotions down. The last thing I needed was to drive Sandy away and into Salem's arms.

"We're all scared." John eased Taylor out of my grip and transfer her to Sandy. "And not thinking very straight."

"I am doing my best." Sandy looked past Taylor's head with tears in her eyes. "I love my daughter."

"I know." I had to blink three times to hold back a tear of my own. "You're a good mother facing a lousy situation."

We all went silence with John moving over to put his arms around the shaking pair and block my view of Salem. Both moves were as much for me as Sandy and Taylor.

Finally, after reviewing a lifetime of perceived mistakes, I broke the hush.

"I just don't want to fail Junior again."

Chapter 60

WE WENT BACK TO THE mattress room and made an effort to lay Taylor down, but she would have none of it. She sensed our unrest, and I had to admit the tension was running at a mountaintop high with a leap off into outer space when Salem disappeared a few minutes later.

I realized what had happened, and I waved off my turn to take Taylor and darted out the door. I found nothing in the next room with an eye sweep and charged on to the next. All the rooms proved equally empty, and when I reached the front door, I turned back into the house to get Sandy and John.

I didn't have far to go.

They had followed me with Sandy entering the exit room as I turned and John carrying Taylor a step behind. Without saying a word, they read my fear and nodded in agreement. We were just about to make an exit when Salem came back in from the outside.

She gave us all a look going from face to face, starting and ending on mine. Then without a word, she held up a roll of toilet paper and spun it around an up-pointed finger.

"You had to go outside?"

"A girl does what a girl has to do."

"Not sure I want to."

I am not sure if it was Sandy being female or my shock for not considering the oblivious that had allowed her to take the lead. But for once, I was more than happy to let Sandy carry the conversation. Tonight I had seen nothing but conflict running between me and Salem, and did not want to add to it.

At least not over the restroom arrangements. We could always work it out by using a corner in one of the empty rooms. Or taking a look at the expression on the face of our single resident of the house, we could go outside.

Me personally, I was going to hold it.

I looked to John, and from the slightly pained expression on his face, he was mulling over the same situation and perhaps regretting his choice of an extra dessert.

Good thing I had skipped mine, but maybe I would have been better off with a couple less Coke refills.

Somehow I knew even before I checked Sandy that she would be in full-form squirm. She had had an extra dessert and perhaps more refills than me. From the clench in Sandy's body and pain on her face, the last refill had taken effect.

"How far away from the house do you have to go?"

"Just somewhere toward the edge of the woods." Sandy flipped the fluttering roll toward Sandy. "There is a rather nice stump just a short way up in front of the house. It will help in maintaining balance while hovering."

I rolled my eyes toward heaven and signaled off a thank-you about the gender of my birth. This conversation had already covered far more ground than I was comfortable with.

"Is it safe?"

"Not if you lose your balance." The question had been aimed in my general direction but answered by Salem, of course. "I have a limited amount of clean clothes and no washing machine."

"John and I will stay right here by the door." I gave Salem a look just short of complete irritation. "And if anything happens, we can be right there in no time."

Sandy smiled nervously and clenched the roll of paper to her chest. Putting it off only made the urge grow stronger.

I knew that for a fact.

My body was screaming for the same kind of excursion once Sandy was back, and John's feet shifting hinted at similar condition.

"While you three consider your options on necessary hygiene"—Salem plucked Taylor free of John's grip—"I am laying Taylor down on a mattress. She is too exhausted for your games."

I almost put a stop to that.

But we did have the only door covered, and going out a window with Taylor in her arms did not seem a likely move. I am sure we would have heard some telltale sound or at least a whimper from Taylor. And Salem might be quick, but I didn't see her out running a well-trained member of our armed services.

And counting Sandy, we had two of them.

I watched Salem disappear into the next room without following and turned back to Sandy.

"Go, I got a feeling we might be following your example when you get back." Once Sandy was out the door, I turned to John. "Who's next?"

"We could both go at the same time." John snickered. "There is plenty of room, and after being in Iraq, I am not that shy."

"Sounds good." And feeling the tension beginning to break, I had to add my smart-assed comment, "But don't peek."

About then our conversation was ended by a shrill scream from outside, and I didn't wait to see if John was answering with a jab of his own. I flung myself out the door and found Sandy on the other side of the stump about forty feet away, struggling with four of Father's goons.

Sandy was ripping at one as he tried to gather in her free hand but was only getting a set of blood welling scratches for his effort. Her other arm was being controlled by a second goon while the others were trying to lift Sandy off her feet. They were having limited luck, but Sandy's best efforts could only hold them off so long.

I took this in during my first three steps in their direction. Then I was halted by a second squeal. This one came from behind me and was much younger.

John took another step before joining my turn around.

This time, our sight was greeted by an even worse sight then Sandy's struggles.

Salem was falling backward out the window into a fifth goon's waiting arms.

She had my granddaughter clamped tightly to her chest, and I could see Taylor was putting up a struggle of her own.

Taylor had pulled her face away from Salem's chest and was squealing out a cry for help. And even wrapped in a blanket, I could see a foot slamming into Salem's rib cage in an effort to break loose.

But none of it was getting Taylor free.

I had been duped, and now I had to make a choice with no time to think about it.

Chapter 61

"TAYLOR!"

The name screamed in my head, either imagined or from a spirit unknown.

Or maybe not so unknown.

"Take care of Sandy." I planted my hand firmly in the middle of John's back and shoved. "I'll get Taylor."

I didn't wait for John's response but pivoted to charge the spot where Salem was making for the woods. I felt the painful pop of muscles in my lower back, with my very first step. And I could have sworn someone from hell had decided to play "stick it to the old man with a red-hot poker." To make it worse for me running they had missed a few inches to the right.

The stab of pain brought my view line up into Salem's face level at the edge of the woods. Our eyes met and locked, and in spite of the lack of light, the heat of Salem's expression came through full force. I expected it to be hate or fear but realized it was a stranger one either asking for help or questioning my strength to do so. I am not sure which. Then the look turned saucy to full-out dare, and with a tuck of Taylor's head in under her jaw, Salem was off and running into the woods.

The pain had slowed my charge for what seemed like forever but in reality only by a micro-moment. I was into my second and third step before Salem's turn into the forest, and had actually gained ground on the loaded-down girl.

I think with Salem carrying Taylor, I might have gotten to her before the chase could have become more than a sprint. But her companion made no move to follow the pair. Instead, he stepped forward to stop me, going into an old-fashioned grappling stance. There was little doubt he planned to stop or at least slow me down enough for Salem to disappear out of sight and sound range.

I had nothing against him, but no one was going to slow me down. I jerked the double-bladed ax free from the stump as I went by and slammed it headfirst into the goon's face.

Neither blade touched the man's flesh, but the flattened wood holding the blade in place did. It thudded solidly into the space between the goon's eyes, and the brow seemed to spread out in a gushing explosion of blood and bone. His head jerked back more than half a foot, but the body never moved from the neck down. It simply folded down on itself as I pulled the ax away.

Swinging it down to my side, I found the ax surprisingly well balance. It had nowhere near the drag you would expect from such an awkward-looking weapon.

The blade was a single piece of iron, but unlike the molded blades of today. This one seemed to be a beaten piece of metal from the forge. A forged blade beaten by a master forge until it was beyond razor-sharp and more weapon than tool.

Stranger yet, it was almost liked the ax belong in my hand.

I had only one real problem with the ax.

It was not supposed to be here.

I had checked the yard earlier, and all the stumps, including the one I had grabbed the ax from, were empty. Another time or place I might have overlooked the ax, but not tonight. I had checked out the stumps extra carefully looking for anything out of ordinary, like a hiding goon. An ax handle would have stood out like a football fan at a soccer match.

There was no way I could have missed it.

But I wasn't going to worry about it now.

I had a whimpering six-year-old to save, and if this ax helped, so much the better.

Chapter 62

BY THE TIME I REACHED the edge of the forest, Salem was out of sight. To amplify the darkness of the brush-laden landscape, the rain returned with a thundering flash of lightning. This time, it did not come down in the sheets of the earlier downpour, but it still came down hard enough to sting the face.

Within a dozen strides, the footing under my tread had become slick and unsure. I was in danger of falling with every step, but at the same time, I dared not slow down. I was chasing Salem by the sound of Taylor's whimpering alone, and with the sound of the rainfall added to the night, it was just that much harder. If anything, I would have to step up my rate to avoid losing contact.

I shifted the angle of my pursuit as the next whimper came a little to my left. The shift brought my head in contact with a low-hanging branch. It was not thick enough to crack a skull, but the brutal contact did bring out a few stars.

The dizziness only added to the misery of pain stabbing through my back. Salem's dare had brought up enough adrenaline to overcome her companion with the ax, but it was short-lived and draining away fast.

A misplaced step rolled off a rock, and again I started to go down. Only a stab down with the ax saved my balance at the heavy off-balanced lean mark and let me push back up. Now as an extra pleasure, I got to run with the added jolt of a twisted ankle to help me along.

The next three whimpers were all directly to my front and getting louder.

It gave me a reason to both keep going and tighten my grip on the ax handle. I could feel its potential to create damage flowing up my arm. A good thing for me, because when I caught up to Salem and Taylor, someone was going to pay a price.

A painful one with a lot of damage.

Chapter 63

T HE WHIMPERING CAME TO A sudden stop, but I didn't need
it.

With my last stride forward, the haze of rainfall burst
forth with the glow of swamp gas, eerie and uneven. I knew it held
Salem and probably a lot more, mostly evil. But I didn't care.

It also held Taylor.

My next two strides were more leaps than steps, and they
brought me into the edge of the haze and hell.

The area encased by the glow was treeless except for a single
giant wall-like tree frozen in place against a rock face rising into the
mist. It looked as if the far half had never gotten a chance to grow,
being halted instead by the stone. But it didn't matter. The front half
made up for it.

It was huge, running a width match able to my Ranger bumper
to bumper, and flowed out into the clearing at least as much. It had
misshapen branches and knot holed surfaces beyond counting. So
many of them a blind man could have used them to dream up a hundred faces, all of them ugly, and all of them outlined by the blooms
and veins of the Witch Rose.

They came from everywhere—to my right, left, and almost
right between my legs. Snaking through the knee-length grass of the
clearing and climbing up and over the tree like the arms of a clinging
lover.

They were not so lovely now.

Right in front of the tree stood three figures. Well, two standing
figures and a smaller one being held with her arms out to me.

Taylor was the only one I was worried about. Her face was
stricken with terror. I doubt if she could have released another

whimper if our lives depended on it, and my mind flashed through a thought questioning the origin of the other cries. At least the last few, where the pitch had slid a few notes deeper.

But I didn't have time to question that.

Taylor's fingers were curling out to me, begging for help. If she had stretched them out any further, they would have pulled both her arms out of their sockets. They might have already been popped, the only thing looking more strained were Taylor's hips joints. I think Taylor might have added an inch in length trying to reach free of Salem's grip.

Yes, Salem was there.

She claimed a spot directly between me and the tree, restraining Taylor on one hip and giving me a look. At first, I would have called it a challenger. But such aggression would have put Salem leaning forward to maintain balance on the balls of her feet. Salem was leaning back as if to maintain a grip on Taylor, but I knew she could have done with one hand standing on her head.

The look could have been a dare, less than a challenge but more than a neutral. If so, I could understand the look as a final statement of chosen sides and daring me to choose as well. After all, my situation would be simplified with Salem as a known evil.

Yet dare did not feel right.

It was a matter of Salem's hackles not being up. There was no ridged stiffness holding Salem's back in a ramrod stance. And where the jaws should have been locked tight, I saw softness. A trait I found leaning more to sadness than anger.

The look might have been pleading, but that would not have fit Salem's position of power. From the very first, Salem had come across as the strong individual above the need of aid, and asking for it now would change the whole question of her chosen side again.

Right now, I didn't need the confusion, especially with Father standing to Salem's left. It was the side away from the hip maintaining a seat for my straining granddaughter. You would think by now it was only fair that things would become clear cut as they dealt with the Father.

At least I thought it was Father.

Gone was the Santa figure of the town. The hair had gained back the darkness of youth, and his body had stretched out long and lean, gaining at least six inches, probably more.

Father looked more like a man of thirty than one of seventy.

The question of son or nephew passed before my eyes but did not come to roost. There were the eyes and essence of evil telling me this was the real Father.

Father had transformed himself, but not for the better.

Chapter 64

"YOU SHOULD HAVE STAYED WITH the others."

"You should have left my family alone."

"Family." The letters of the word rolled off Father's tongue as a snort. He tilted the head back as if to give himself a better angle for looking down his nose at my world and finished. "Six months ago, you never knew woman or child existed."

"In my heart, I knew of them." Or at least hoped I had. "And it doesn't take time to make someone family."

"Really." If the words were any oilier, Father could have used them to comb his hair. "And how would you know?"

"Because I have been a real father."

Father's eyes flicked to Taylor and Salem, helping to crack a smile more evil than the grin of a crocodile. When they came back to me, I knew what he was going to say before it slithered out, but that didn't lightened the stab.

"Yet it is my sons who still live to serve me."

I twisted the ax within my fingers as I rolled up the sleeves of my shirt in my mind. For the first time, I noticed the feel of craving in the wooden shaft, and it took my mind back to a world of their making. Probably done without meaning, they still had been the likely shared time between father and son. A precious commodity people like Father would never be able to cherish or value.

"But it was mine who shared a life of trial and error, joy and tear, and most of all the give and take of a family."

"I'll take my thirteen coven sons over a sniveling memory."

The force of Father's words tightened my grip on the ax.

Or was it his words.

It felt more like a heat of a familiar grasp from times long ago when a son held to his father's fingers for support making his first step.

"Thirteen, I count eight." Two, who were backing Father up to his left as if guards while the other six formed a standing arch in the knee-high grass on my left, ready to step in between me and Salem. "Perhaps the others are no longer serving."

"They come now." Father smiled with the crack of brush behind and to the right of me.

I shifted to expand my sight line as three of Father's goons cleared the brush and entered the glow of the clearing. They lacked the number 5 Father had expected, and only one stood tall. He came in supporting a limping comrade while the third followed, dripping a dark fluid from several deeply carved scratches.

"They come short."

"They can be brought back." Father twisted as an emotion on fire, heated and twisted ugly.

"With a face destroyed?"

I again felt the crunch of the bone shattering under my ax blow and knew my opponent was one of the missing. The other I credited to John and Sandy, hoping they had escaped injury themselves during the inflicting.

"Or mine can be replaced." Father's hand came up to halt their advance into the glow. "Can you say the same for your son?"

I looked from Father to my granddaughter, reaching silently to me. Played out beyond speech, Taylor's eyes were struggling to maintain a hold on my awareness and perhaps losing their grip.

Could Taylor be a replacement for Junior?

Taylor had only been in my life for days and was not even a boy. She could no more carry my name on, then she could relive the missed years we had passed over. All she could do was grow up, get married, and provide some other man's name a lifeline to the future.

I did not even have any real proof Taylor was my granddaughter. Only the word of a desperate woman who had yet to offer up proof of a testing or written statement. Should I risk a fight, perhaps my life, for a child who could never be my son?

I looked to Taylor's arms weakening with a settling of the hips into Salem's hold. I measured the eyes of the captors, skipping Salem's, already knowing they would show the same doubts as my own.

Then I rolled over the only word that really meant anything. Granddaughter.

Chapter 65

I COUNTED OUT THE ODDS AGAIN, getting thirteen to one with me being the only one armed.

Again, I checked the ax, broad-bladed in an old style, more weapon than tool. Two big *C*s of hammered metal held on to the shaft by wood hammer out flat at the top and tied to the shaft with strips of metal banded in *X*s back and forth to stabilize the ax head in place. It was marked with symbols either random or older than the gods of Celtic times.

Thinking back to my moment of gathering up, I remembered neither the bands of metal nor symbols being a part of the ax. Then it had carried the look of modern times fresh out of the hardware store.

Thinking I had missed the ax on my first look was bad enough. To have mistaken if for a hardware item was something else. This went beyond strange.

But I also had to admit, being strange had become the norm lately.

About then the movement in the corner of my eye became more daring, and without thinking, I shifted the ax into a single-handed grip. Without really looking, I swung it out into a wide arc, ending in contact with one of Sandy's assailant.

I felt the ax bite into flesh without slowing down, hitting bone with the slightest of jars, and then continued on in the arc. Before I realized it, the blade had passed all the way through Father's goon and almost dragged me around with the follow through until my back was to Father.

With a backward stagger, I maintained an awkward balance while somehow keeping both Father and the goon in sight. Not that the goon lasted much longer.

My blow had almost severed him in half, but he didn't bleed. He just sparkled away like a Fourth of July firework display.

Yet I knew he could bleed; the goon had come in dripping dark fluid from Sandy's defense.

And the one I had smashed in the face?

He had dropped with no fancy shimmer or sparks, just a crunch of dissolving bones. How could this one be different? If it wasn't the *who*, it had to be the *when*, *where*, or *what*.

When went out with the lack of different in time from his arrival and the recent scratching. The *where*, I ditched because of the blood still dripping when the goon had stepped within the clearing.

The *what* could be from the size of the cut or the change of my ax from wood chopper to war ax. I ran the fingers of my left hand down the shaft as if playing a piano, but no music came out. This was a tool built for pure destruction, not beauty.

And somehow in my heart, I knew the ax was the reason for the sparkles.

Chapter 66

"THE AX!"

"A garden tool, nothing more." I shifted focus quick enough to see Father twitch away Salem's hand and snarl a silencing sentence.

"Running out of zombies." I let the ax go into a one-handed grip and let its normal weight rock the shaft back into a pointing arc. "If you lose many more, who will you have left to protect you."

Of course I couldn't help from following Father's eyes traveling around the clearing counting heads, and hoping there were no more in the brush. As it was, I could not see myself taking on the ten who were left. And that was counting on Salem and Father staying neutral during any physical combat.

"You're just a mortal fool." Father spread out his hands. "My sons are the least of my power."

Okay, not what I wanted to hear. Santa Claus had already transformed himself from a merry old fat man too old and short to be a danger into a younger version of the boogeyman from the fears of my childhood. I almost found myself checking the new Father out to see if he would fit under a bed or in the darkest corner of a closet.

"And?"

I made no secret of my look to Salem.

Maybe with a little luck, my directing of the word at Salem would keep the self-style preacher busy with his own love of importance. Given time, I could hope John's military training would bring him to the clearing. His presence would really help my odds even better if he brought a raging army mother with him.

"My Salem, she has her uses."

Father's hand reach missed its intended mark on Salem's arm, but whether it was from his own mistaken judgment of distance or the slightest shift of Salem's body, it was impossible to tell. Personally, I like the idea of Father's forces showing any split at all, with one between him and Salem being at the top of my list. Of course, I would have also liked the arrival of an armed squad of army rangers coming to my rescue, and I did not see that happening.

"But Salem is nothing compared to the power of childish potential." Father held out a clenched fist to the rain and wind, swirling a hell storm of fury just inches from our glow-lighted clearing. "There is true strength. The 'what might be' locked in the depths of a child's seed. It can take away the hindrance of an old man's years and give me strength to bend my future into an eternity."

"You're nuts" rocked on the tip of my tongue, but the words did not come out. There was too much information coming out beyond my limited knowledge. If felt like something out of one of the movies Junior and I had enjoyed sharing on a Saturday night. They were total fiction except in a child's mind.

"And those powers can only be challenged by a mother's love." Father brought the fist down against his chest. "And being male, you have none of it."

I needed to answer, but Father had nailed the truth.

The truth of a weakness, I recognized, but could never overcome.

Yes, I could be a father, but never a mother.

And perhaps that was the reason my son had gone to Iraq and never returned.

Chapter 67

GLANCING OVER MY SHOULDER SCRUBBED away those layers of hope.

Without the whimpers, I might never have found this clearing. Without their aid, it would have taken an ocean-sized dose of dumb luck to get here. And any trail I left would have either been washed away in the rain or hidden now in the dark. There was no such thing as moonlight, and the eerie glow around me didn't stretch more than a few feet beyond my sight. How could I expect John or Sandy to find this place?

How could I expect anything?

Even with my recent lucky blow, I was badly outnumbered by Father's people on their home ground. If I took a single step toward Taylor, I would put either the two injured goons of my right or at the very least the end guy from the half dozen to my left behind my sight line. With a little movement, they could have me spinning back and forth like a broken-necked fan in a brace trying to watch a tennis match.

Sooner or later, one of them would get in a back stab.

And then?

"I want my mommy."

I heard Taylor's whimper, and like it or not, I had to meet my granddaughter's eyes.

They were heavily drooped and showing a look of "You let me down" I had seen so many times before. The birthday Junior had checked the mail, expecting a promised gift from his mother, but getting the slap of an empty mailbox. Junior had tried to explain it away by reminding me the promise had been for Christmas still months away. Only Christmas became a repeat performance.

She promised, and I took the blame.

Didn't matter.

She was a mother and had the advantage of bonding in the womb.

Me?

All I had was a million nights of holding my son's head against my chest as we rocked away the nightmare of a baby's mind. And the pride of watching him spank a curveball into right field on a little league team where everyone else was missing it. Maybe if they had cared less about winning like Junior, they could have just relaxed and done the same.

Mothers were born with motherly love; all we fathers got was our world wrapped around a daughter's smile or son's grin. And if really unlucky, you got your hearts ripped away and traded for a red, white, and blue rag that was supposed to pay a father off for twenty years of being there.

And now, I was just a grandfather, old and hurting.

My sciatica nerve had helped forced an early retirement, and running up a rain-slicked hillside had forced the nerve into working overtime. The results ripped my body with waves of pain, two degrees beyond hurting. If I had any sense of well-being, I would have given up this chase long ago.

Extreme cold had joined the enemy's side years ago. And tonight's August rainfall would have been cold even for December. Legs, hands, back, and fingers were all cramped and pained. I am sure I could have found a part of my bodying not hurting, but it would have taken a thorough search by someone with more patient than me.

I found myself in the beginning of a chin drop. The same type used by the French as they readied themselves for the drop of the guillotine, but I never finished it.

Instead, I felt the lift of a finger under my chin. The same movement I had used with Junior when the world had used a hammer to drive his chin down. Guilt, the pain of being dumped, you name it. Even when I could not fix the problem, he knew I cared.

That care kept us close even when Junior was a world away fighting desert heat and Arab terrorists. I could not remember how many times we had talked about his dreams for a postwar future. One filled with children, kids he wanted to raise.

And maybe he cared now either is spirit or memory.

I hoped so.

Because it sure helped me bring my sagging chin back up when Taylor screamed the one word which had the power to wipe away all the weakness of age or pain.

"Granpa!"

Chapter 68

TAYLOR HAD USED THE LAST of her strength in a sudden surge toward me and must have caught Salem by surprised. Her only hold was at the ankle level, and Taylor was in a half stand, about ready to topple forward or kick free.

Not sure which, because about then Father caught Salem with a backhanded slap. It hit her high in the shoulder and drove her off balance even further than Taylor's surge. Salem was forced to take a step and caught the foot against an extend root rising up from the clearing floor. Without Taylor's weight, Salem might have regained her balance, but with the added burden, Salem went down hard.

Inside, I winched in dread of my granddaughter being squashed. But before my muscles could twitch and begin for a dive that would never come in time, I watched Salem spin her body in midair. She brought herself under Taylor and protected my granddaughter from any major injury.

I am sure the breath would be knocked out of both Taylor and Salem, but my granddaughter landed screaming. Salem hit quiet, but bounced, spitting out a hiss. Since I did not hear the crack of breaking bones or rip of tearing flesh, I hoped for both to be uninjured.

A moment later, I was not sure if I would ever hear anything again.

Whatever had held back the storm at the edge of the clearing gave way. Icicle drops the size of walnuts slammed into my face. They were accompanied by winds that must have howled here from the wilds of hells and brought broken twigs and ripped leaves with them. Together, they seemed to score my skin off and drive nails into my joints.

The falling of the storm barrier was not the only change.

What had been a steady glow from an unknown source was now a flickering. First being as bright as daylight and then holding little more light than the after dim of a lightning strike. It would have been the perfect time for Father's goons to make their move, but they too were caught up in the change.

Even Father seemed taken aback by the moment. For a full heart rotation, Father stood before the tree, with his arms outstretched and studying the sky as if looking for a sign. Yet it was Father who brought himself back to the moment, first looking down at us as if we were little more than an afterthought.

He strode over to Salem and grabbed the back of her neck with one hand using it to haul the girl to her feet. Salem did nothing to aid Father's jerk up and had to be in pain. But no cry came out, and I had only a couple of half-lit glimpses to confirm her pain.

Releasing Taylor would have given Salem a better chance to help herself up and reduce the pain. But Salem would have none of it, swinging Taylor into a tighter grip away from both Father and freedom. The movement again added a flicker of doubt in my mind against what I knew was Salem's true character.

"Once Father had hoisted Salem to her feet," he switched his attention back to me while shaking the pair like mother cat and kitten.

"You! Do you realize what you have done?"

"No, and I don't really care."

"You will." Huge drops of spit flew with his words. "And then I will finish what I started, by adding Taylor's mother to the offering."

I shook off some of the water pounding into my eyes and tightened the grip on my ax. For some reason, it felt as if two other hands were gripping the ax over my own, adding the strength of heart I had been missing since the burial of my son.

Growing taller yet, Father must have stood almost seven feet in the shifting glow of the night. Without changing his grip, he lifted woman and child off the ground and stabbed the finger of his other hand out at me.

"Kill him."

Chapter 69

THINKING FOR ONESELF HAS ADVANTAGES.

While Father's sons were digesting his order, I took him at his word and moved.

I pushed my ax into a two-handed swing and strode in the direction of the two to my right. Any other attack would offer them my back, and while not a military genius, I had watched quite a few action movies. They might not know it, but they were going to be guarding my rear with their dead bodies.

Or without them.

My swing caught gimpy full in the rib cage, basically ripping him in half and setting off a shower of sparkles. From the look on his face, his own death was just registering in his mind as my blade nicked his comrade.

The second goon had been the more aware of the two, ducking down and away from my swing. It almost saved him with only the width of my blade prevented the escape. The sharpened tip of my ax scraped across his forehead, splitting it open but to no great depth. I figured the best I could hope for was a stunning, but I did not get even a seeping of blood.

What I did get was much more startling.

The skin edged apart, and a glimmer of light emerged. Within micro-moments, the cut had spread wide enough to engulf the head, and as I didn't need to see the rest, I turned back to the heart of the clearing.

It had changed a lot during my brief charge.

Father still held Salem by the back of the neck, but he had lowered her enough for her to stand on her tiptoe. Not the peaceful type, Salem hissed out her anger and might have scratched out the coven leader's eyes, but she was too busy holding on to my granddaughter with both hands. Taylor was not making it any easier for Salem, setting off a howl of her own and squirming away with all of her six-year-old muscles to get away.

The goons?

One of Father's bodyguards had stepped up to his side as if guarding against my next charge. The other had drawn out a cache of weapons to arm the remaining goons. Only two had not waited. They had been on the end of the line furthest from me but were now within an arm's length of grabbing my throat.

There was no room for an ax swing, but I managed a pivot under the first one's grasping hands. His speed rush impaled him on the pointed end of my ax blade. His effort to free himself removed the lower part of his stomach and sent him to twinkle-twinkle land.

The second slammed into me with a good old-fashioned football tackle. I tried to lessen the blow but could neither free the ax in time nor twist the body in any positive way. I went down hard, jarring my pain-filled body and sending off a sparkle show of my own. Most of which was contained between my ears.

Not having time to wait out the show, I grasped for breath to fill my emptied lungs and drove an elbow down into the attacker's exposed ear. It rocked him to one side and filled my arm with enough pain to fill the Grand Canyon.

I am not sure how I kept moving, but I feel now as if an added push from above would not have been out of the question. It gave me the power to wiggle away from the reeling goon, and into a roll under a knife flung in my direction.

The flinger kept coming.

I met him with the bent knee lift from my judo days in college and let his momentum carry him over my head and into the brush. Not sure how far he flew, but I heard at least one thud of a tree being banged solidly and hoped for several more unheard.

My tackler had recovered enough to grab at my feet. He got his fingers around one ankle in an effort to keep me down, and it might have succeeded. Only now my hands were free enough to raise the ax, which I smashed down on the grabbing hand at the wrist. The hand came off neatly, and his fingers disappeared from my foot with a poof of flash. I didn't have time to watch the goon follow his hand as I rolled away to the side and on to my knees.

Father's men should have been on me, but they were holding back. I guess having their number dwindle from thirteen at the beginning of the night to five a few hours later would be disturbing.

I took in a deep breath of rain, wind, and air while bringing my right knee off the ground and extending my leg into a stance a bit closer to a stand.

My friends did not like it.

They shifted around like a bunch of sea lions wondering if the orca was waiting in the water below. It was then I realized my knife flinger had been one of Father's guardians. He had given up passing out weapons to use one of them instead.

His partner was still standing by Father, but he had no more compulsion to attack than the other four. A situation Father was not happy with. He was trying to do the double duty on controlling the girls while pushing the man next to him in my direction.

For the first time, I saw a real emotion on one of Father's male followers.

It was stark, naked fear.

Chapter 70

FEAR WAS A REAL BREAKTHROUGH for the goons.

Was I the one causing it?

Or did it come from the more likely Father, a tyrant who had controlled the man's every breath for only they knew how long.

Perhaps with luck, a bit of his terror came from both sides of the question. It couldn't hurt my chances of success to have their minds clouded in conflict over whom to fear most.

I used the ax head braced against the ground to lift my other knee off the ground and into a bend-over crouch. I should have taken it further, but my lungs were still sucking water-soaked air. With my head hanging halfway down, I could see everyone's concern and keep a small part of the flow away from my face. Going into a straight-up stand would have taken this slight protection away.

Finally, Father put an end to the standoff.

He flung Salem toward the tree behind him and grabbed the struggling goon with both hands, one on the near shoulder, the other in the middle of his back. Using a jerk and tug, he threw the man forward in my direction and growled for the others to join him.

I knew the moment of truth was coming but didn't care for the idea. My lungs were still hurting from their loss of breath during the tackle, and dozens of stars flicker around my sight lines as if they really existed. I did not have enough left to blow over a ladybug, let alone fight off five armed goons.

I might have mustered myself for a defensive stance while Salem ran off with Taylor, but that was not going to happen.

Salem had taken up a half curl against the tree with Taylor spooned within her arms. Neither showed much fight, but I was too far away to read their eyes, and I couldn't believe a daughter of Junior's could ever give up.

Of course, it was just as hard for me to believe I was here trying to rescue a daughter of Junior's from a nut case who led an old-time coven. Looking down at the ax head, it would have been easier to believe this was all a nightmare.

I wondered for a moment if you died in a dream was it the same as dying when you were awake? I didn't really want to find out, and I put it out of my mind as Father's remaining goons gathered themselves for a rush.

I came to my full height with a helpful nudge against my lower back. I knew the aid did not really exist but imaging it helped. If this was real, I would definitely need some supernatural help to prevail and survive.

Barely able to see through the pain, I brought the ax up into a two-handed grip across my chest. Four deep sucks later, I lifted the ax up with my right hand and slapped the handle back down against the palm of my left.

"Come on, I'm the good guy." I slapped the ax a second, third, and fourth time. "And good guys always win."

Except of course in real life.

The man with the biggest weapon won then.

Chapter 71

THERE WAS ONLY FIVE LEFT, but they were all armed. Nothing military or even as dangerous as a bow and arrow, but more like farm tools that could be used as weapons. Two of the goons were wielding pitchforks, with another brandishing a single-bladed ax that carried more than a few dings and dents. The guy who looked the most nervous had a pair of mismatched knifes, one a butcher knife, the other more likely used for skinning rats in the local church. Both of them looked to be well sharpened.

And the leader of the five?

He carried a hand sickle, which would have worked equally well as both a seed detacher and chicken-head remover. I couldn't be sure, but he seemed to hold it with a familiarity I didn't like.

Looking closer, they all seemed more comfortable with farm tools than they had with cell phones or iPads. Not in the way a tractor jockey would, but more like the old-time farmer who did everything by hand or with the help of a horse to draw the plow.

"They've lived a long time."

"Longer than they should have."

"Perhaps." Father moved just enough to give me s full view of his windblown hair and half-smile grimace. "But I think you will find they all want to live some more."

"So?"

"At the moment, you stand between them and another decade."

"Me"—I squinted my eyes against the rain—"or my granddaughter?"

Father threw a look over his shoulder to make sure the ladies were in place and then returned his attention to me.

"Taylor is already in place." Father's eyes glittered brightly enough to show across the clearing. "You are just stalling the ceremony."

"I'm stopping the ceremony."

Father threw back his head in a laugh.

"Like you stopped your son's death?"

The comment should have cut me to the bone, especially with me being exhausted and hurting.

But it didn't.

I felt like there was an invisible hand blocking away the words and whispering encouraging words in my ear.

Probably a side effect of the wind and rain rushing into my ears. If it got any harder, it would push me across the clearing to Father and his goons. That did not seem like a good idea, considering they were waiting for me with sharp objects.

"Why not just give me Taylor and creep yourself some other way?"

I hoped Father would count his loses and look for an easy way out. Replacing goons might not be that hard for the mob, but they were a different breed from Father's group. They actually fit the definition of thinking zombie better than goon.

"Taylor is payment."

"Payment to who?"

"To the tree."

Father's smile showed enjoyment only a soulless animal could understand. It was as if twisting the blade of dark knowledge into my confusion seemed to be the highlight of his entire miserable existence, or if nothing else, at least the night.

"You're sick!"

"I am over three hundred years old." Father seemed to stretch up another two inches to stare down his nose at me. "And plan on living three hundred more."

An honest-to-God witch or nut, and did I really want to know which?

Chapter 72

ABOUT THEN, I CAUGHT ON to the fact that Mr. Double Knife was spreading out to the left while the pitchfork brothers were doing the same in the other direction. With a scream somewhere from my forgotten past, I lunged at the pitchfork brothers. They jerked away and fowled each other into a tangle mess of arms and legs.

They would have been easy picking, but getting a butcher knife in the back while doing the picking did not seem like the best of ideas. So as they went down, I shifted into a pivot, which brought the knife bearer darting forward into range of my ax.

My swing brought the ax under his upraised arm and into the rib cage. Even without the strike going all the way through to bring forth the sparkle time he would have been finished. Thinking the number 4, I shifted back to meet the last of the two uncommitted goons.

They were coming at me halfheartedly. Neither of the two seemed excited about coming within striking range of my ax. It probably saved them from the bite of the ax as I shifted my hands and brought the weapon swinging on a return journey. It missed the closer of the two by a good foot and a half as they jumped back away from me.

Only he wasn't spared.

A tiny bolt looking like copper-tinted lightning jumped from the point of my ax. It shot out at the apex of my swing and crossed the gap between me and my attacker. It bounced around on the arc of the lead goon's sickle and then settled into his hand.

At first, I thought it was a trick of light, especially when it disappeared into the goon's hand, but he threw away the blade as if it were a live snake. Only the sickle did not hold the poison; it was already inside.

And it wanted to come out.

The man's face went from terror to pain and then beyond as everything went outward. Not as an explosion but just outward expanding until there was nothing left. The only thing remaining was a discarded sickle and glimmer in the air.

I was not the only one shocked.

The goon standing nearest sagged with his single-bladed ax drooping toward the ground. Behind him, Father's mouth actually hung open without spewing any verbal crap in my direction. And strangest of all, Salem was smiling.

She must have lost her mind.

So far, tonight Salem had been chased through the rain-drenched woods by a crazed old man with an ax, slapped to the ground by a delusional nut case, dangled like a cat, thrown to the ground again, and all the while dealing with a squirming six-year-old who wanted to get away.

To be smiling now?

Salem must have crossed over to land of super-long-sleeved shirts with ties in the back. I just hope she didn't try to take Taylor with her.

The goon and I both recovered from the experience at the same time. He hoisted up his ax and threw it at me, but his grip in the rain was slippery, and his weapon clattered well off to one side.

I pointed my ax out, thinking to deflect his twirling blade to one side before I realized the poorness of his aim. I found out then my pointing came with consequences. Good for me, but bad for the ax thrower.

He took the lightning bolt square in the chest bone. Again, it disappeared into the man, and with a look of horror, the man stopped being.

A clatter to my right reminded me of the pitchfork brothers.

They were back on their feet and doing their best to disen-gage the intertwined prongs of their pitchforks. It should have been easy to get them apart, but the two were in a panic. When they saw me looking in their direction, they threw the farm tools down and turned to run.

I should have let them go, but they had threatened Taylor.

And for what?

Maybe a few more years kissing the back side of the heart-less creature who had dangled my granddaughter like some rabbit plunked from a hat. Taylor deserved better. I deserved better. And most of all, my son Junior had deserved better than to give his life for creatures like this.

I pointed out the war ax, and this time, twin bolts flew across the gap. One hit the goon on the left in his rib cage as he turned to flee; the other was struck in the back, but both received the same payment.

In a moment, they were gone, and I was able to turn all my attention to father and his damnable tree.

Chapter 73

FATHER DIDN'T LOOK IMPRESSED.

"A couple of them were with me from the first." Father spared a half glance back at Salem, telling her more than me, "But I was bored with them, and they can be replaced."

"I thought you could bring them back."

"Why bother?" Father held his hand out like a cup. "This modern world of yours has so many discontented children. Why not offer them a better way?"

"For who?" I sucked in a breath of socked air and wished my chest hurt a lot less. "You or them?"

"Me, of course." Father tightened his cup into a fist. "You and the others like you are little more than fertilizer."

It was not the first time I had been called a piece of shit, but this certainly was a new way to do it. If Father kept it up, he might hurt my feelings, but he had a long way to go. Junior could have told him as much. He had watched his father hand out better insults in my sleep, and I had taken much worse abuse from people whom I actually cared about. Those words taken to heart might have hurt, but I had laughed them off and survived.

And now this old witch from a couple centuries ago thought he could do better.

I didn't think so.

"Well, me and the rest of the fertilizer have kept building a new world year by year . . ." I straighten myself up and thought of some fertilizer filling a hole down in Arlington Cemetery. I would be damned if I let his efforts be undone by an aging asshole. "While immortals like you have come, gone and been forgotten."

Father's smile faltered.

Not in width or depth, but in background. The strained muscles of his neck lost their uplifting joy and tightened down into a stressful set. The clenched fist loosened enough for the intimation to dribble away, leaving hanging in the air the empty gesture of a really old man.

"You have no idea where my power comes from."

"Or you, mine."

"A misguided belief in good." Father was grasping out to regain his control of the situation. "I quit worrying about good before your grandfather's birth."

"That's your mistake."

Father's grin held no warmth or cold, just nothing.

"Humanity's mistake." Father opened his hand to wave back at the old misshapen tree whose only effort for beauty were tiny white flowers with a crimson trim, and a million of them could not have made up for the ugly. "My tree lives off your so-called strengths."

"Your tree . . ." Keeping Father's mouth in gear was buying me time to reach out for the resources I had gathered over my lifetime. Those I had stored up while teaching a boy to swim, seeing my daughters hug their own children tight, and being told I was loved. "Or your owner?"

"My tree." Father pounded his chest and flipped his reach upward toward the sky. "Unlike the red savage who gave up the tree's secret. I stayed in command while he burned at the stake in my place."

"The secret?"

"Nothing you can use." Father settled back flat-footed.

"Nothing that exists outside your warped mind."

"You want to play," Father's grin widened, "while praying for help which will never come? How humanlike and vain."

"Any worse than believing in your Christmas tree?"

"My tree." I noticed Father's careful drop of the word Christ but was not sure if it was the religion or the good it stood for he avoided. "This tree has lived off the potential of mother's love since before the first humans crawled out up unto their feet to become hunters."

"What?"

Confused and dazed wasn't something new to me, but what I was coming to believe was even worse. Being dumb had it advantages, but probably not now.

"Don't you understand yet?" Father shook both hands in front of my face to push across the point. "A mother's love. The reason a she bear stands off a pack of wolves to protect her cub and why the female of a species gives herself over to the pain of childbirth. When in reality, the offspring is seldom worth such an effort."

I could argue the point but didn't want to interrupt Father on a roll. So I filed it away and kept listening.

"The potential from such a commitment is beyond measure." Father dropped his voice down to a whisper barely heard about the pounding of the rain and roar of the wind. "And it is all there stored in the soul of an untapped six-year-old."

Father stepped to one side to give me a clear view of Taylor huddled in the grip of Father's pet. A bitch no better than the beast she served. Right then as Father completed his rant, I promised to make her pay a price equal to Father's.

"Taylor's end will give up the potential of her mother's love to my tree." Father's stance went neutral as if reaching the end of a lecture in his college class. "The tree will share this power with me as I search for yet another feeder, thus keeping us both immortal."

"Don't count on it." I hoisted the ax into a warrior's grip remembered from my ancient German past and got ready to strike. "Because in a moment I am going to split your skull wide open."

Chapter 74

NOTHING SHOULD HAVE BEEN ABLE to stop my blow.

I took six running steps and then stepped into it with a combination of Paul Bunyan the lumberjack and Conan the Barbarian. It sung through the air with several times the power of my earlier blows, but . . .

Father reached out and caught the handle inches below the blade and stopped my swing dead.

It wasn't possible, but Father did it.

He held the blade dead still above our heads, and then slowly dragged it straight down between us. As I stood there in shock, he placed his other hand between mine on the handle.

"I told you"—Father began a slow push of the ax toward my heaving chest—"I have the power of a mother's love at my fingertips."

I felt back to a cold misting day in Arlington, where my tears had mixed with the rain. I hadn't been able to say goodbye then, and I could not do so now.

With a familiarity breed from long night of butting heads over bedtime and finalizing hugs when one of us gave in, there came a warmth and strength. The ax stopped moving in my direction.

"Too bad. . ." I gritted my teeth to add, "I have something stronger."

"There is nothing stronger."

"Wrong." The ax quivered and then jolted a quarter inch in Father's direction. "I have a father's love, a parent's love."

"Used." The muscles of Father's neck budged out like the twisted rope of a giving rope as he halted the ax's quiver. "Mine is untouched."

"Mine is tempered." I held off Father's new attack as if it were little more than a summer breeze trying to blow over an oak. Seeded with the first smile of a newborn child, forged in the heat of their late-night fevers, watered with the tears of their first heart break, and bonded hard with every shared "I love you."

"Nooooo!" A hint of fear flickered deep behind the hate of Father's glare. "It is not enough. It can't defeat me."

"It will." I felt Junior's hand pushing mine forward, edging the ax forward now ever closer to a chest laboring even more than mine.

"Salem!"

Without looking away from Father, I saw enough of Salem in the background to know she would be no help to Father. She had tugged Taylor's head up under her chin and displayed a grin of pure satisfaction.

"Why should she help you?" A gloat filled my chest, and I leaned into the push, driving the ax blade into the surface threads of Father's buttoned shirt. "When have you ever shown Salem any love or even affection?"

"Cats are animals." Father's words were labored, but he did move the ax back and inch. "Property to be used."

"Cats love their young, and that gives them a soul." I pushed the ax back, cutting into the material and scraping the skin. "Which is more than I can say for you."

Father tried to wiggle off to one side, but I would not let up. The blade eased into the flesh, and a dark fluid almost bloodlike eased out.

"You can't!"

"I can."

There was a quivering as if the tree was pushing out toward the father, and for a moment, he held fast.

"I won't die."

"You will."

The words were mine, and every other parent, no matter the title—father, mother, uncle, aunt, mentor, or most important now, grandfather. For this moment, they all lent me their strength, and I pushed the ax into and through the Father.

He gasped out a breath of sheer stench, smelling of hate and evil. Nothing I can describe and nothing I ever wanted to smell again.

I thought it was his last breath, but Father sucked the stench back in and tightened his death grip on the ax. Despite my best effort, the ax began to back out. I threw myself forward into a renewed effort, but it only slowed the blade's draw back.

"I can't die." The words bubbled up from a lung no longer able to function. "The tree won't let me."

I glance up and found Salem clutching Taylor to her chest and staring in terror. Whatever her allegiance, Salem had not expected this.

Only a demon from hell could have, or . . .

"Move!"

Salem ducked away as I jerked loose the ax to unleash the smell of hell's sewer. Before it could force me reeling back in repulsion, I pivoted around Father's stationary body. Then with a war scream from the hearts of my German ancestors, I brought the ax whirling into the tree.

The ax did not bite into the solid feel of wood. Instead, it sank full blade into an evil of rot so old the animals before man knew it. Shaking away a shock of disbelief I had no time for, I pulled the ax free. With a quick change of grip, I drove the ax into another spot on the ancient trunk.

This time, the ax sank beyond blade, almost bringing my upper hand inside the tree. Crimson-rimmed flowers twisted at my feet, and Father let loose a scream you couldn't hear with your ears.

It came from the pain of a thousand mothers who had gone childless to feed the tree. Some were animal, many were human, but all had died soul tortured beyond my grasp of reality.

It hung there unheard long after Father had given up his hold on living. Dying with the tree and leaving nothing for my third strike to destroy. Even as I pulled out my blade for a fourth hit if needed, the growth was crumbling in upon itself. Within moments, there was nothing remaining but a blotch of stained rock with wilted blossoms pulled back against its wall.

Chapter 75

"P ops!"
"Salem?"
"I didn't expect."
"Me to win."

"No, this." Salem's hand came off the back of Taylor's head to point at nothing and everything all at the same time.

Once free, Taylor's head bounced loose like helium-filled balloon suddenly untied.

"Granpa!"

Taylor followed her single word with a push off to free herself from Salem's grip before the stunned creature could react. I thought Salem was going to make an effort to reestablish contact; instead, she let her hands fall to her sides, and Taylor came to me with a swirling mop of wet hair hiding her tears.

"Grandfather, I was so afraid."

"Me too." And I wondered if my change of titles came because of the moment or a new closeness. Perhaps one caused the other.

I hugged Taylor tight, warmed by her love even with the cold rain still throwing a bruising at my back. Only the physical presence of Junior could have made the moment better.

"No matter Father's words, Taylor is your blood."

I looked past Taylor's shoulder to Salem.

She was now on her feet, and I had to bring my gaze up into her face. She could have been trying to complete the offering, but I saw no hate in Salem's face. It just showed an irritation aimed at the water soaking her silver locks.

"Doesn't matter. Blood or not, Taylor is mine."

"As a granddaughter?"

"As a future." I brushed my lips gently against Taylor's damp hair. "Junior's future."

"She won't carry his name."

"Taylor will carry his spirit."

"Is that enough?"

"No." I make no attempt to hide my pain from Salem. "But it will have to do."

Salem's face exhibited the know-it-all smile of a cat. Then without saying another word, she made to slide by me, but I was not done.

"Whose side were you on?"

"My own." Salem's eyes took on a blankness I could not begin to penetrate. "But I am not unhappy if my actions helped to spare Taylor."

"How many others have you failed to save?"

"Beyond your count." Salem's words came out but the merest breath from hiss and spit. "But remembered in my mind each and every child of innocence and how they died."

"You could have run away."

"My kind have graced many a mantle." Salem's words dripped with the venom of forced heritage. "We have served as a focus until released, either willingly or through death."

"Whose death?"

"Hopefully the master." Salem licked at her lips. "But all too often our own."

I looked at scared soil around the rock.

"Not this time."

"No, not this time."

Chapter 76

"**S**TILL WANT TO SPLIT MY skull?"

Salem stared openly at the ax held clutched in one hand against Taylor back.

"Not today."

This clearing had seen too much death. And while I could not trust a soul who had given up so many others to hell, I would not add another death to the toll. At least not today.

"I am too tired for any more skull chopping."

As we talked, the rain eased back into a trickle, and the wind eased down to a hard blow. It was like an audience trailing out of the theater with the trailer still going. I just hoped there was not a hidden scene waiting to jump out.

"Ready to guide us back?"

"No." Salem stepped around me nearer to the forest. "With the death of Father's storm, your way will be lighted by the moon."

"Through a forest I don't know." So much for any goodness with my luck I would fall off a cliff.

Salem wiped away the last of the dampness covering her face and knelt down to pick up a wilted twist of vine. She fingered it like a piece of cat crap before lifting it up for my inspection.

"Follow this, and it will lead you to the houses."

"Your home?"

"My prison."

I came up to my feet as Salem dropped the vine back to the ground. In spite of my earlier words, her shoulders hunched as if expecting a blow. I took it in and would have left without saying anything more, but I had to ask.

"John and Sandy?"

"I honestly don't know." Salem pulled back the silver hair into a rope for water stripping. "But Father's sons gave no sign of success with their return. If I were a predictor of future, I would say you will find John and Sandy waiting for you."

"At the house?"

"At least until daylight." I looked around at the sky, which was clearing above my head. It showed no sign of daylight, and it felt like this night had gone along forever. "There are several hours left, at least four."

"Will they be all right?"

Salem shrugged. "Their attackers came back in bad shape, at least those who came back."

Wasn't much of an answer, but I realized it would have to do.

I wiggled to a standing position without releasing my hold on Taylor or the ax. Once up, Salem held out the vine, and I took it between the fingers of the hand holding the ax against Taylor's back.

"I wish you luck."

My exhausted granddaughter's head shot around at that. "Salem."

"What?" Salem came close enough to chuck a finger under Taylor's jaw but still kept an eye on my ax.

"You can't leave us."

"I can." Salem's expression again showed blank. "I am no longer your pet."

"You were never my pet." Taylor reached out to lock a grip around Salem's neck, but came up short by inches. "You were my friend."

Salem's chest welled up as if full or too tight to hold down. And I could have sworn there was a tear forming in the corner of Salem's eye.

"And sometimes friends have to let friends go."

Chapter 77

AND THEN SALEM WAS GONE.

It must have happened during the blink of my eyes.

"Will I see her again?" Taylor seemed to have blinked at the same time, because as she turned to me, she sported a look as dumbfounded as mine.

"I don't know." I looked around as if somewhere I should see Salem or at least something slinking around the edge of our clearing. But there was nothing except the words I offered Taylor. "But if you carry her memory, Salem will stay with you in spirit."

I took a moment to settle Taylor into a one-armed carry on my hip before slinging the ax over my other shoulder. I thought about leaving the weight behind, but it seemed to carry a bit of Junior I was not willing to give up.

By keeping my head down, I was able to follow the vine without having to pick it up or run the ugly string through my hands. The flowers had all died, but even if they had still bloomed, the white blossoms would have held no attraction to me.

The rain had stopped, but the ground was still wet. I could have jumped up and down without making enough noise to startle a feeding deer or slumbering child. And from the deep breathing in my ear, I was proving that on the latter.

I forced myself to stay alert.

I did not want to twist an ankle on the broken undergrowth. I was already struggling with more pain than a retiree had a right to suffer. Most guys my age would be sitting in front of a television, watching a game a baseball, but not me.

I was marching through the woods with a back screaming out the words to an opera in the language of the pinched nerve. Bad part about it was that the rest of my body was only a step or two from drowning out the opera with a heavy metal screech of its own.

I guess that is why I never heard the tackle coming.

It came out of the dark and slammed into me on the ax-carrying side. The blow numbed the length of my arm, and my fingers let go of the ax. It spun away in one direction while I went flying in the other.

Even as my toe lost contact with the ground, I realized there was only the choice of breaking my fall or protecting Taylor. I did the right one, spinning myself to keep Taylor on top so that I did not land on her.

The fall still knocked the breath out of my Taylor as her startled cry cut off with a grunt. My mind kept thinking Taylor was getting introduced to the hard knocks of life in some very large doses more than anyone deserved in the first six years of their life.

But before I could think any more, the force of the landing ripped into my mind. The music of the strings, drums, and even the thundering beat of the heavy metal guitars was gone. There was nothing left to my being except pain and a dull remembrance of a need to protect.

The need got me to a knee. But only in time to hunch over Taylor's body as Father's last son came rushing at us. He was holding my ax up over his head, and I could think of no defense or dodge to prevent the coming blow from ending my life.

No matter how much I loved, in the end it looked like I was helpless to prevent an end to Taylor's life, just like I had been helpless to prevent the death of my son, and there was no reason to blame myself for it any longer. I had done my best as a father and grandfather; there was nothing else I could do.

Sometimes evil wins.

Chapter 78

SOMETIMES, BUT NOT THIS TIME.
I wanted to beg, not for me.
But for Taylor, with Father gone, there was no reason to offer her up. It would just be killing for killing's sake.

But a beam form the moon above showed me it would do no good to beg.

The man's eyes were empty except for a crazed glow. It might have been caused by pain, hate, or even just a snapped mind, but it told me there was no reasoning with the man.

I made an effort to avoid the blow but had nothing left to pull Taylor away with me. After everything tonight, I could not save or forsake my granddaughter. The only thing left was to die with Taylor in my arms.

Only Junior's spirit must not have been done.

Even as the man began an overhanded blow with the ax and Taylor jerked up to release a scream of fear, it all changed. A silver ball of fur came launching from the brush with a spitting hiss splitting the air around us. It hit the man under his upraised ribs and sent him spinning into the underbrush for a second time tonight.

The next sound was a death scream, and in my heart, I knew the man would not be coming back a third time. It took a long moment to take in the scene, which was left behind.

I was on my hands and knees, covering a sobbing child and taking in the sight of a large silver cat hissing and spitting at the spot of the recent death scream.

It was larger than a house cat but smaller than a lion or tiger. It was sized more like a leopard but reminded me of neither the dark or spotted ones I had seen in the zoo. She seemed to carry an exotic flavor more often carried by the snow or clouded leopard, as deathly as their African cousins but with their ugliness hidden under a layer of beauty.

Finally, I drew myself together and made it up to one knee. From there, I gave the cat a look and fumbled my granddaughter to her feet and into a hug. The cat took it in and sat back silently to lick at her paw as if she touched something dirty.

Taylor sobbed a few more times but then drew in a deep breath and asked, "Is he dead?"

"That or down the hillside so far we will be gone before he can get back."

"Not dead?"

"Stay here, and I will look."

Taylor would have none of that and grabbed my leg as I moved forward. I thought to point out the cat would protect her, but the pussy was also moving forward with me.

Even with my living leg iron holding the pace to a shuffle, it took only a few steps to see over the twig-shattered bush my attacker had crashed over. And a single look told me what I wanted to know.

His fall had taken him through the bush and onto the ax. Lucky for me but unlucky for him, the blade must have twisted loose from his grasp and landed blade up. It had split his breastbone in two and came out through his spine. He had probably been lucky to get off a death scream, and one look told me he would not be getting out anything more.

The cat had moved up beside me and resumed the body cleaning. When she realized I was staring at her, she blinked twice and turned her attention to Taylor.

Seeing the man dead and the cat looking up, Taylor let go of my tattered pant leg and bent down.

It took my all to hold back an instinct to grab Taylor up. After all, this animal had just shown off the perfect example of a predator's kill and probably outweighed my granddaughter by double.

Taylor had no such fear. She placed her arms around the cat's neck and hugged it tight.

Even in a choke hold, the cat did not react much, simply putting her paw down on the ground and gazing up at me like she was bored.

I shook my head and let out the breath I didn't know I had been holding. I should have kept it in.

Chances were I had broken a rib or maybe two, and the knee I had ignored was twisted real bad to say the least. Getting down the hillside in the dark was not going to be easy, and carrying Taylor might be impossible.

I looked to the cat.

"I don't suppose you could play Lassie?"

Yep, as I expected, my question did not rate an answer, just a blank stare telling me where I could go.

Well, at the very least, I would need the ax to use as a crutch.

I turned back toward the body and found it wilting away like the blossoms I had been following. It already looked dried out enough to be an ancient mummy, and it was getting stronger by the second.

After everything else I had seen tonight, it didn't bother me.

The absence of the ax did.

The crack of a broken branch coming up the hill did so even more.

I all could think was, *You have got to be kidding.*

Hadn't I gone through enough already?

Better yet, hadn't Taylor gone through enough?

At least I had the big cat on my side.

Right!

When I looked back, my protector was slipping away into the brush.

She stopped once and looked back.

A goodbye, a "See you later," I am not sure what she was saying. But I did know I was getting no more help from her tonight.

I watched the cat disappear into the brush and then turned to face the second branch crack coming up the hillside.

Not sure what I had left to give, but I was going to give it for my son and his child.

Chapter 79

"**H**EY, OLD MAN, CAN YOU hear me?"
Junior!
Only Junior had ever called me the old man.

I wanted to fall down and accept my call to heaven, but I couldn't. I had to protect Taylor.

Speaking of which, Taylor came off the ground and began moving toward the voice.

"John!"

"Taylor?"

"You got my mother?"

"She is back at the house"—the crack of branches became a thunder of a hurrying soldier—"locked up safely so no one can get to her."

About then, John came into the light of a moon beam and stopped to grin at me.

"Pops!"

Son, if not by blood, by the moment.

Chapter 80

JOHN TOLD ME LATER THEY had no idea what to do after I ran off. They had scared off the attacker after John had more or less ripped the head off the one holding Sandy's leg. The rest had scattered with the crack of their friend's neck and gone in three different directions.

John had thought to follow, but which one, and Sandy was in no condition to chase through the woods. She was sporting an ankle twice its normal size.

In the end, they had retreated to the house and prayed for my success.

I guess they had more faith in me than I did.

The situation had stayed like that until shortly after the end of the rainfall when Salem had come back.

Staying well out of reach, Salem had yelled instructions on how to find me and Taylor. At first, John had doubted her words, but Sandy had pointed out it might be their only chance to help and insisted he follow them.

John missed the rest, but Sandy filled me in after we reached the house.

It seemed after John's departure Salem had told Sandy how to get back to roadway, where she would find a title for the car in the glove compartment. It would have Sandy's name on it and be perfectly legal, given to her as a gift from a now missing Father.

Salem told Sandy whatever else she found in the car was also hers.

Whatever else turned out to be enough cash to get Sandy moved to Michigan within a twenty-minute drive of my house. There was enough left over to send both her and, in the future, Taylor to college.

I take Taylor with me when I go to Arlington Cemetery every Memorial Day. We stand over Junior's grave, and I remind her that a father's love will always stay with you. I hope she understands and it helps to make up for his absence.

Me?

And I still check my backyard from time to time to see if any silver cats have moved into the area.

None so far, but you never know.

And when I check?

I get the feeling someone else is looking over my shoulder, staying with me until it comes my time to join him in the hereafter.

About the Author

C. T. HEINLEIN WAS BORN in Bay City, Michigan, and was part of the second graduating class of Bay City John Glenn High School.

From there, after a short stint at the US Air Force Academy, he attended Central Michigan University, earning a BS in education.

A wrestler in high school, he went on to do judo in college, using this love of sports to teach and coach a number of different sports in Kuwait, Liberia, and upon his return to the States, Texas.

As the father of two and grandfather of one, he learned the true meaning of "If you are close enough to be a friend, you're close enough to be considered family." Now his family includes one-time students, many friends of his kids, and a collection of the best people this world has to offer.

This family helps him survive the loss of his son Charlie Junior in Iraq and the strength to keep writing and dreaming.